The
Thirteenth
Trick

Also by Russell Braddon

THE NAKED ISLAND
THE YEAR OF THE ANGRY RABBIT
COMMITTAL CHAMBER

RUSSELL BRADDON

The Thirteenth Trick

W·W·NORTON & COMPANY·INC

NEW YORK

Copyright © 1972 by Russell Braddon

FIRST AMERICAN EDITION 1973

Library of Congress Cataloging in Publication Data
Braddon, Russell.
Deadly Finesse
I. Title.
PZ4.B7979Mo [PR6052.R25]   823   73-665
ISBN 0-393-08375-6

PRINTED IN THE UNITED STATES OF AMERICA

2   3   4   5   6   7   8   9

CONTENTS

WEDNESDAY: HALF PAST TWO

She had chosen a stretch of road where she could see each on-coming car for a quarter of a mile: to thumb the right car, the right driver.

She wore her brother's faded jeans – their slightly extruded zip gaping an inch at the top – scarlet shoes, a voile shirt with the three top buttons undone, its tail knotted across her bare midriff, and a purple, floppy-brimmed hat. Swinging from her left hand was a satchel. Her right sat on her buttock, its thumb hitched into the back pocket of her jeans: waiting for the right car, the right driver.

Eight passed. Six without a glance, two with more than a glance – both rejected with a toss of her floppy purple hat.

But the ninth, she felt, as soon as she saw it at the end of the momentarily deserted road, was the right one; and as the driver's head and shoulders grew more distinct behind the windshield, she knew it.

Unhitching her hand from her buttock, she waited. Then, insolent thumb extended, swung it twice across her slightly extruding zip. And stood motionless as he passed her.

Thirty yards on he halted, unlatching the door. Didn't open it: just unlatched it. And wasn't looking back. She liked that: liked confident men. She strolled to the car, swinging her satchel. With her hip she pushed the door wide and, stooping, thrusting her head inside, asked : 'Going far?'

'Far enough' – glancing into the rear vision mirror: noting the empty road. 'Make up your mind.'

'Domineering, aren't we?' she jeered. But slid in beside him.

It began to rain, and he switched on the windscreen wiper. Then, turning towards her, placed his left arm along the seat-top behind her and his right hand on her belly.

'Don't waste time, do you?' she commented, but without rancour.

Not bothering to answer, he withdrew his hand and kissed her. Eyes closed, she failed to notice that his were open; and that his right hand had gone to the glove box.

WEDNESDAY: TEN PAST THREE

As perversely as it had started, the rain stopped. Whereupon the sun shone, making leaves and grass blades, and
droplets on the windscreen, glitter. But Mark Gifford was
used to the glare of sun off water. Unblinking, he swung
his car out of the narrow country lane and through the
gateway of his brother's cottage.

Though the garage at the end of the concrete drive was
open, his brother's Morris 1100 stood outside. As he pulled
on to the lawn beside it, and switched off his ignition, he
frowned. Not that anyone unfamiliar with him would have
taken it for a frown: not so slight a furrowing of that
smooth forehead, which suntan made even smoother; but
briefly he frowned. Then, reaching behind him, took a
suitcase from the back seat, got out of his car, slammed its
door and, straight-backed, casually dressed, strode across
the soggy lawn.

The glass door at the side of the cottage was closed and
the big living-room behind it empty. Sliding the door
open, he stepped inside. More loudly than he had intended, he called: 'Robbie?' – standing feet apart, the
heavy suitcase held easily away from his leg.

'Who's that?' From the front of the cottage. At which
he relaxed.

'Mark, you twit,' dropping his suitcase, stretching, pulling off his driving gloves. 'Who were you expecting?'

9

'Oh ... Margot and Rudy, Margaret and Tony. You know, the usual mob.'

'You in the bedroom or the heads?' A cistern flushed. 'Don't answer that.' He glanced round the familiar room. At the far end, the kitchen unit; on either side of the fire place, chintzy arm-chairs; leaning against it, a fencer's sabre; in front of it, the sofa; on the chimney piece, the electric clock he had given Robbie for Christmas; and, flanking the clock, a photograph of himself in his officer's uniform on one side, the transistor radio he had given Robbie for his birthday on the other. An electric clock his brother wouldn't have to reach awkwardly high to wind : a radio his brother obviously never used, or it would be on the low table beside the farther arm chair, along with his bottle of whisky.

Still – it was the thought that counted.

Crossing to the fire place, he switched on the radio. He was twenty-five and he disliked silence. Which the latest chart-topper shrilly pierced as Robbie wheeled himself into the room.

If anything, Robbie was better looking than his brother, his shoulders even broader, his clothes as informally fashionable, and his complexion as smooth. Whereas Mark's habitual expression was one of amiable candour, however, his was bland.

'Vulgar word that,' he rebuked, deftly manoeuvring.

'What?'

'Heads. Why can't you say bog like everyone else?' Almost as an afterthought, he held out his hand, which Mark shook.

'Hello, Robbie.' For all its casualness, Mark's greeting was affectionate. Perhaps too affectionate, because Robbie at once withdrew his hand, looking him up and down.

'God you're brown,' he complained. 'And unpunctual! Five you said –' glancing at the clock, which said only a quarter past three. 'Or is that stupid machine on the blink again?'

'No,' began Mark, glancing at his watch, 'it's—' But Robbie, having wheeled himself to the chimney piece to examine the clock, cut him short.

'Not on the blink : going. On electricity, of all things. Which I'll never understand. I mean' – swivelling round to face his brother – 'how can the same stuff make clocks tick, kettles boil, fridges freeze, radios talk and television look at you?'

Mark laughed. Always, after each voyage, each time he came home, the same thing. This same few minutes of facetious fencing; of parrying any attempt at intimacy. 'You really want to know?' he demanded, tossing his driving gloves on top of his suitcase.

'No. But when all the kettles in Britain suddenly start screaming pop, like that bloody radio, and the TV sets freeze, and the clocks boil, don't say I didn't warn you.'

'How are you, Robbie?'

'Fine.' But reached irritably and ostentatiously high to switch off the radio.

'You sound a bit. . . .' Mark let the sentence die.

'It's been a long time,' Robbie explained, with a show of contrition. 'And I got myself into a state – cleaning.'

'Well, next time, leave the cleaning.'

'And then you get here almost two hours early, and catch me with my pants down. . . .'

'I'm sorry.'

'Metaphorically *and* literally down.'

'Relax, Robbie. My fault for being early. You had a lot to do in the house; and you had to go out. . . .'

'Did the shopping. Steak do for dinner? Have to, anyway, 'cos that's what we've got. How was Sydney? And why, for Christ's sake, don't you sit yourself down?'

Even for Robbie, even at the beginning of a reunion, it was staccato.

Dumping himself in an arm-chair, Mark said simply: 'What's wrong?'

At last Robbie smiled. 'You know me,' he shrugged. 'I don't really mind this thing' – slapping the wheels of his chair almost affectionately – 'so long as I can kid everyone into *not* wondering how I manage the bog. The bog's the bit that really bugs me. It's so. . . . Even you I try to kid. Anyway' – looking sociable – 'how come you're early?'

Hesitating only a second Mark answered: 'Woke up too late to go to the dentist, so I mucked about in the flat and then set off for here.'

Robbie seemed not even interested. 'Good trip down?' His tenseness had vanished.

'Deadly. Sheeting rain the last few miles and a terrible hitch-hiking bird.'

'*You* picked up a bird?' Robbie looked both disconcerted and amused; and Mark wished he hadn't mentioned it.

'A raging nympho,' he muttered.

'You, who're always on about hitch-hikers and why can't they pay their own way and what a cheek they've got asking strangers to transport them for free? You gave a girl—?'

'I know, I know. But she was lying at the side of the road in this monsoonal ruddy rain and I thought, Christ a hit and run job, and pulled up; and before I could even open my door to look, she'd hopped in.' Robbie laughed. 'Said it always worked and please would I drive her to Aylesbury where she had to meet her aunty! Outside the post office.'

'Sounds reasonable,' commented Robbie.

'She was a man eating blonde, well below the age of

consent, with eyes made-up like a whore's and an I.Q. of minus infinity.'

Robbie shrugged. 'Chance like that, I'm surprised you were early.'

'Man eating birds are not my scene.'

'Are any birds your scene?'

Back to the old subject, thought Mark. 'I know,' he conceded. 'I'm twenty-five, unattached and I never talk sex! Well, neither would you if you were at sea with a mob who talked nothing else.'

'You mean', corrected Robbie gently, 'neither would I if *you* were the one in this chair, virtually a eunuch like me.'

Mark met his brother's melancholy gaze without flinching. 'I don't talk that talk to you because you're the brother I've always worshipped,' he said simply.

Too simply for Robbie. 'Quite right too. I'm extremely worshipful! By the way, did I tell you I'd been picked for the Games?'

'The Olympics? No!' Mark was delighted. 'For archery?'

'Archery, the javelin and fencing.' Though he threw it away, as if it were absurd that he of all people should represent Britain's paraplegic athletes in three separate sports, there was a glint of ferocious satisfaction in his eyes. Satisfaction, Mark realized, not at being best in three separate sports, but at having denied three separate rivals the place to which each had aspired in an Olympic team.

For an instant such ungenerosity made him uneasy. Surely one place would have sufficed? But then he remembered the Robbie of his youth : the superb athlete; the joyous competitor; the medical student in his final year who had been certain of a place in England's squash team, until a mid court collision had sent him sprawling across the polished yellow boards – and left him a cripple.

But still a competitor. Though Stoke Mandeville Hospital was celebrated for its fighting spirit, it had never produced a more implacable fighter than Robert Gifford. For which, disregarding the shattered hopes of all his rivals, one had, Mark acknowledged, to admire him.

'Robbie,' he congratulated, 'that's great. You might have written and told me.'

'Didn't I?' – looking vaguely surprised : ignoring the fact that he never wrote.

'How long've you known?'

'Ooh,' shrugging, 'a month; maybe six weeks. I lose track of time.' It was an uncharacteristic, if oblique, reference to the differing attitudes of the disabled and the fit, implicitly resentful, for all its offhandedness. Aware that he had erred, however, Robbie made swift amends. 'And if I didn't write, I'm sure I meant to. . . . Of course, what the Electricity Board *should* do is invent a machine that takes letters down as you think them. I mean' – wheeling himself into the middle of the room like an actor taking centre stage 'who *needs* an *electric* clock? That's the trouble with science : keeps applying itself to things we already have and ignoring completely the things we need.' Frivolously, he made his chair pirouette; and waved a disparaging hand at the power point beside the fire place. 'Do you reckon,' putting a finger in his ear, 'you'd get a letter if I plugged myself into that?'

'Yeah. From your solicitor telling me you'd fried.'

They were happy now; playing with words, suspending reality.

'I might just steam,' countered Robbie, 'or light up.' He headed for the kitchen unit. 'Feel like a cuppa?'

'Thought you'd never ask.'

'Sorry there's nothing stronger. Got to keep to me budget, though. Occasionally.'

Mark rose from his chair. 'I brought some whisky—?'

Kettle in hand, Robbie whirled to face him. 'Sit down,' he rapped. Then, visibly controlling himself as he filled the kettle and switched it on : 'Just sit yourself down again and talk to me.'

'It's only out in the car.'

'Well, leave it there : you've bought me enough.'

'Balls.'

'Them, unfortunately, you can't buy. But everything else you have : from this piss-elegant chair to my magnificent car and my humble abode that must have cost you a bomb.'

'It wasn't my money.'

'The old man left it to you.'

'For us. He. . . .' About to say, he meant me to look after you, Mark changed his text abruptly. 'He knew what a twit you were about money.'

'Nonsense,' retorted Robbie. 'He left you his money because you were his favourite, which proves what a discriminating parent he was; because he was a solicitor who didn't want twenty thousand odd frittered away by a second lot of death duties if I predeceased you; and because he knew I'd predecease you by forty years at least.'

'Now who's talking nonsense?'

Before answering, Robbie pulled open a drawer and carefully took out cups and saucers. 'One day, probably sooner than later, my kidneys'll pack it in. The paraplegic's occupational hazard. I know it, you know it, the old man knew it.' From a lower, deeper drawer he took a teapot. 'So, very sensibly, he left everything to you.' He placed the teapot beside the kettle and turned his chair to face his brother. 'And very generously you've spent a lot of it on me. But enough's enough. All I want is to see you occasionally – when you can spare the time.'

'Robbie, I look forward to it.'

Turning back to the kettle, Robbie poured hot water

into the pot. 'I'm surprised you bother,' he muttered, swilling the pot, warming it.

'Oh Robbie!' Mark walked to the wheel chair and, standing behind it, gripped his brother's shoulders. 'I look forward to seeing you when I'm home. I look forward to sending you letters when I'm away. I look forward to hearing from you *while* I'm away. Not that I ever do—'

'Blame the Electricity Board!'

'Okay, I'll blame the Electricity Board. But let's have no more of that "I'm surprised you bother" crap. I like it here.'

'Must be the thought of all those blondes thumbing lifts on the way,' Robbie bantered, filling the teapot. 'Though if I were you' – more soberly – 'I'd concentrate on brunettes in future.'

'You mean they still haven't caught him?'

Indifferently Robbie shook his head. 'The countryside littered with murdered blondes, and apparently they haven't a clue.' Opening his refrigerator, he took out a carton of milk.

'Sure you don't want a whisky?' Mark asked him.

'Quite sure. Take it back to your scruffy mates in your London pad.'

Mark hid his disappointment. 'Dunno that I want to really. They're all bores.'

'You could move.'

'It's comfortable, and cheap, and I'm hardly ever there.'

'Well' – pouring tea, somehow indicating disapproval – 'it's your life; but a flat with three other blokes in it, and sharing a bedroom when you are there, is hardly my idea of a love nest.'

Again the old subject. Change it. But not too obviously.

'Dirty things, nests.'

'Lair, then.' Presistent; and testy.

'Lairs are smelly.'

Robbie slammed the teapot on to the draining board. 'You're just *not* to be pinned down, are you?'

'As to what?' – defensively, because he'd lied about missing an appointment with his dentist. His teeth were as flawless as they looked. What he'd missed was lunch with his girl friend – with whom he'd had a corrosive row, about spending three of his six days' leave with Robbie. But that he couldn't tell Robbie. Not the Robbie whom the nurses of his student days had called Doctor Kildare; whom girls no longer even noticed.

'As to what you think, what you do, what you hope to do, who you like—'

It had to be stopped. 'I think about my job; I hope to become a Commodore; and I like you.'

Again the tension passed. Smiling wryly, Robbie mused : 'The strange thing is, you always did.' He passed a cup of tea.

'Nothing strange about it.'

'Your parents did adopt me.'

'Which means they chose you. Me they unsuspectingly made – and were stuck with.'

'Does that bother you?'

'Never thought about it. Does your being adopted ever bother you?'

Now it was Robbie's turn to change the subject. 'I'm sorry. Been a bastard, haven't I? It's just that. . . . You know, after six years, you'd think I'd be used to this.' He banged the wheel of his chair. 'But there are still times—'

'Drink your tea.'

They sipped, thoughtfully silent : until the silence between them became almost tangible, like a wall topped with shards of glass.

'When you're finished,' Mark suggested, saying the first thing that came to mind, 'I'll set up the target.'

A flicker of enthusiasm lightened his brother's grey eyes:
then died. 'You'll be bored stiff.'

'Try me,' grinned Mark, picking up the target that
leant against the wall opposite the fire place and carrying
it to the open garden door. 'Go on: go get your bow and
arrows and try me.'

So Robbie wheeled himself past the telephone on the
table in the hall, past the bathroom on the right and the
doorway to the garage on the left, and into his bedroom:
while Mark carried the target to the end of the long lawn
and set it up, against the hedge, exactly forty nine yards
and two feet (Robbie had once made him measure it)
from the doorway.

In which Robbie now appeared, turning his chair sideways, positioning it so that the wheel nearest the target
lay along the crack between the second and third floor
boards: so that he would be shooting from exactly fifty
yards.

'All right?' Mark shouted.

'Fine. How's the wind?'

'Isn't any.'

'Okay. Stand clear.'

'I wouldn't insult you,' staying where he was, a few
yards to the right of the target.

'Do what you're told. Nowadays my neck gets stiff and
my aim can be hairy. What'd people say if I killed you?'

Surprised, because Robbie had never asked him to move
before, and perturbed, because Robbie had never before
mentioned a stiff neck, he retreated a few yards and
watched his brother draw the bow he himself found it
difficult to draw, hold it steady at full stretch for fifteen
seconds, which he himself was unable to do, and shoot.

After the last shot, Mark plucked six arrows from the
target and walked back with them to Robbie. 'Not bad,'
he said. 'You got a bull.'

'A gold,' corrected Robbie. 'And you're right, it wasn't bad : for someone who's allegedly a master bowman, it was bloody terrible.'

'Not if he's got a stiff neck. How long've you had it?' Ignoring the question, Robbie again drew his bow to its full stretch and loosed off an arrow. Then five more.

Again Mark collected the arrows. '*Two* golds,' he reported. 'You're getting better.'

'Not better enough,' grumbled Robbie. 'Bring the target inside.'

WEDNESDAY: HALF PAST THREE

His bow across the arms of his chair, Robbie watched Mark stroll towards him, the target held single handed on his head. He's strong, he thought, and good looking, so why does he keep coming? Hero worship still? Who are you kidding? And why's he smiling? What's there to smile at, for Christ's sake? On the other hand, if you've got teeth like that, and a tan to show 'em off, why not? Dentist, he'd said.

'How's the toothache?' he asked, as Mark, stooping, replaced the target against the wall.

'Just a check-up.' Had there been a pause before he straightened : before that easy answer? 'Your neck bothering you?'

'No. It's just that shooting from indoors doesn't *feel* right. What I should do, I suppose, is go to Stoke and practise properly.'

'Why not?'

'You've just arrived!'

'I could come with you.' The ever accommodating Mark.

'Forget it,' Robbie told him, turning away.

'Look,' said Mark, 'you want to practise, don't you?'

'Yep.'

'Only you don't want me to come with you?' Looking more perplexed than hurt.

Choose your words, thought Robbie. 'Would you believe me,' awkwardly, but with that self-deprecating smile that never failed, 'if I said you put me off?'

Mark's face cleared. In a school play he had been confident and good, until his eyes had met those of Robbie, who was sitting in the third row, between his mother and father. At which he'd dried, and had to be prompted. 'Remember the last school play?'

'You were the best Macbeth I ever saw.'

Mark laughed. 'I'm the only Macbeth you ever saw.'

'That hint of a burr: very clever. Don't tell me *I* put *you* off?'

Mark nodded. 'So what time'll you be back?'

'Six,' said Robbie promptly. So promptly that Mark realized he'd intended going to Stoke Mandeville all along. Typically, though, he'd manipulated things so that his departure seemed to have been forced upon him. Well, that was Robbie.

'I'll put your things in your car,' he offered, reaching for Robbie's bow.

'No!' It was not only angry, it was uttered with such hostility that Mark recoiled, shocked. Robbie forced himself to sound more reasonable. 'I do everything for myself, Mark; you know that.'

Yes, Mark knew that. Since the day he'd first visited Robbie at Stoke Mandeville, he'd known it. 'Get the hell out of that chair and STAND,' a physiotherapist was screaming at Robbie as he arrived. He'd wanted to box her ears, screaming like that at a seven stone wraith. A wraith through whose pathetic frailty shone a pale child-like beauty. A sick, beautiful child of a man who, after five operations, from the chest down, without his spinal brace, was a rag doll; whose once magnificent legs, without their calipers to lock them, were hopelessly unhinged.

But rag doll Robbie, white with distress, had still fought to get out of his chair.

'Stand!' the sadistic girl had snarled; and Robbie, groaning, had frantically, unavailingly, struggled to obey. Until Mark had stepped forward to help him. When he too had snarled.

'Don't you dare! Till the day I bloody die, don't you *ever* dare,' Robbie had snarled; and had stood.

Which had only been the beginning.

Yes, he knew Robbie did everything for himself.

'Only being sociable,' he apologized.

'Sure.'

'Like opening a door for someone else to go through first.'

'I know. Sorry I snapped. But everything's such a battle, once I let anyone help with anything, I'll soon let everyone do the lot. Put me to bed, clean the house, get me in and out of the bath, get me in and out of the car. . . And God, how I hate getting in and out of that car.'

'Ever thought you may be doing too much?'

'The day I can only do less, I'll take those,' vowed Robbie, indicating the small bottle of phenobarbs that sat on the table beside his whisky.

'Don't say that.' It was a subject Mark hated.

'It's my life,' said Robbie, who had no dislike of death.

'Not if you end it.'

'If it stops being interesting, why prolong it?'

'Depends what you call interesting.'

'Winning,' grinned Robbie, who had had enough of his brother's orthodoxy. 'Preferably gold medals at Olympic and Commonwealth Games! Wonder if they'll go on holding Commonwealth Games when finally they wake up to the fact there's no longer a Commonwealth?'

Mark looked surprised. Since his accident, Robbie's interest in politics – domestic or international – had been nil. He listened to no newscasts and read no newspapers. 'That's unlike you,' Mark commented.

'It's the Games I'd miss, not the Commonwealth.' Another reference to the emptiness of his life, apart from sport.

'Maybe' – wondering how much a companion would cost – 'you shouldn't live alone?' Mark suggested.

'And maybe,' scoffed Robbie, 'my father shouldn't have broken my back when I was four, so that twenty years later a bit of a bump on a squash court'd land me in a wheelchair. But' – gesturing fatalistically – 'he did. And if he hadn't, I'd never have been put in what the authorities euphemistically described as "care"; and if I'd not been put in care, your parents would never have adopted me; and then I'd never have been taught to speak properly, or had a good education, or played squash, or known them and grown up with you; so maybe everything turns out for the best in this crummiest of all crummy worlds – and you should leave well alone.'

'I didn't know,' Mark murmured, 'you'd been taught to speak properly.'

'First thing the parents did when they got me – sent me to an elocutionist.' He laughed. 'Don't think they could understand a word I said. Nice of 'em to never have told you, though.'

'We could easily get someone to keep you company.'

'Actually, kiddo, I prefer it alone. Serious, aren't we?'

'A bit.'

'Well, if I'm going, I'd better go. What'll you do?'

'Have a kip.'

'Sleep well then' – wheeling himself to the open doorway. 'See you at six.'

'Practise hard.'

'That, little brother, I will.' And propelled himself up the lawn, out of sight.

Glancing restlessly round the room, Mark moved to the fire-place and switched on the radio; took his cup to the kitchen unit and felt the teapot – which was cold; picked up Robbie's chest expander and, grimacing, found himself able to stretch it only four times; slashed the air with Robbie's sabre, and felt suddenly foolish; went to the lavatory; returned and, opening his suitcase, took out a paperback; sat down to read it and found he had read it already; got up, walked to Robbie's whisky bottle, and found it empty; heard Robbie slam the door of his car and start the engine; listened till he could no longer hear Robbie driving away up the narrow lane; then walked up the hall and out the front door.

To return, two minutes later, through the garden door, carrying a satchel, a floppy brimmed purple hat and the body of a blonde in jeans. Depositing the dead girl on the sofa, he dropped her hat and satchel on the floor, stepped three paces backwards and, still facing her, lowered himself into an arm-chair.

WEDNESDAY: TEN TO FOUR

His features taut but expressionless, he sat immobile, until he became aware of the dead girl's eyes. Beneath green lids, and through mascara-ed lashes, they were staring at him. He rose and covered her waxy face with her purple hat. Then unknotted her shirt and, pulling it down, concealed the blood-seeping wound beneath her breast bone. He returned to his chair.

That he was planning how to get rid of her would have been obvious to anyone watching him. Or not watching him; clearly he couldn't just leave her lying around. But as to what he was planning, or what his thoughts about her were, the closest observer could have drawn no conclusions at all. Except that he would do nothing rashly.

The radio played on and he sat tense in his armchair, marshalling his thoughts.

'First,' his housemaster had always admonished him, before examinations, 'be sure you've read and understood the question.' Well, the question here, as he understood it, was *How would you dispose of the corpse of a girl in such a way as to attract no suspicion to yourself while clearly indicating that she is the fourth victim of a murderer at large known as the Motorway Maniac?*

In other words, how to dispose of a body cautiously enough not to be caught, yet recklessly enough for it to be the unmistakable work of a man whose previous victims had all been blatantly dumped in front of police stations?

'And never forget the clock,' his housemaster had invariably admonished him. 'For each question, there's only so much time.'

Time! Was anyone waiting for her? Or even, at this very moment, reporting her missing, instigating a hue and cry? He leapt to his feet.

'Never flap,' his first skipper, a Welshman, had constantly admonished him. 'Because, if you do, you'll not be able to think straight. The thing to do, boyo, is always to identify the problem and then to think back to the solution laid out for that problem in the relevant book. Almost everything's there, in the relevant book.'

So which is the book relevant to the problem of the disposal of corpses? he asked himself with bitter irony; but, suppressing the instinct to panic, made himself think.

If anyone was expecting her anywhere, there might be a letter in her satchel. Tipping the satchel upside down, he emptied its contents on to the carpet in front of the sofa. Sunglasses; a steel comb; an Iron Cross on a chain; a long blonde wig; a small purse; a photograph of a wild haired pop singer inscribed *'To Janine Talbot, with thanks and best wishes, Randy Horn'* – and on the back of it, in what Mark presumed to be her own handwriting, her name and address; cosmetic items; two keys; and a bottle of perfume.

Hell, the stopper had fallen out and perfume was soaking into the carpet. He ran to the sink, wet the dishcloth, returned to the carpet and, kneeling, rubbed vigorously. In his right hand, the dishcloth : in his left, the unstopped bottle. Which now was slopping the last of its contents over his trousers.

Forget it : it'd dry out. But wipe your finger prints off

the bottle and drop the bottle into the satchel. Taking the dishcloth back to the sink, he rinsed it, put it back where he'd found it, dried his hands and drew on his driving gloves. No more finger prints.

No letter either: so maybe no one was waiting for her. But still only a limited amount of time. Robbie would return in an hour and three quarters. And when Robbie wheeled himself into the house he would *not* be expecting a corpse on his sofa.

Wheeled himself.

'And if it's not in one of the books,' his skipper had constantly admonished him, 'you'll have experienced it yourself, somewhere, some time.'

A wheelchair was the answer.

Now that he knew what he had to do, he moved quickly and coolly. First through the door on the left of the hall, into the garage, whence he returned with Robbie's old chair; then into Robbie's bedroom, from which he returned with a travelling rug.

Lifting the girl from the sofa, he sat her in the wheelchair, wrapped her fingers round the end of the arm rests, and tucked the rug round her legs so that her flaccid knees were bound together and her scarlet shoes concealed.

Her head, however, lolled.

Back to Robbie's room, from which he returned with a neck brace. Five minutes later, her head was erect, her chin high. Too high, with that dishevelled hair and those staring eyes. He combed her hair, slid on her sunglasses – and stood back to survey his handiwork.

Even behind tinted lenses, her eyes remained conspicuous. Unblinking, that was why. Close them? Worse. Ah – the hat. Carefully he positioned the hat so that the floppy brim would shield her eyes from the gaze of anyone approaching her.

Perfect.

Now for himself. Which was easier. Simply cease to be himself.

Removing his shoes, slacks and shirt, he took a pair of jeans from his suitcase and pulled them on; added a white T shirt and a pair of plimsolls from Robbie's bedroom; hung the girl's Iron Cross round his neck; adjusted her long blonde wig on his head; and examined himself in the bathroom looking-glass.

Horrible; but effective. Except his eyebrows were too dark for blonde hair and the hair itself too girlish at the back. With a rubber band from Robbie's desk, he transformed his girlish tresses into a hippy's horse tail and, borrowing Robbie's horn rimmed polaroids, masked his too dark eyebrows.

He switched off the radio, put the girl's belongings back in her satchel, slid two pounds into the pocket of his jeans, placed the satchel on top of the rug covering the girl's lap, glanced round the room – checking – and wheeled the chair through the garden door, up the lawn to his car.

Where he opened the door, unwound the window and lifted the girl with her rug-swaddled legs on to the front seat, holding her upright with his left hand through the window while he closed the door with his right. She looked quite comfortable, leaning half against the back of the seat, half against the door.

Folding the wheelchair, he carried it to the driver's door, dumped it on to the back seat and got in beside the girl.

'I'm sorry, love,' he told her as he drove through the front gate and turned into the lane, 'but until we get where we're going, I'll have to talk to you. No disrespect : it's just gotta be done so's people'll think you're alive. Specially when I'm getting you out of the car and into your chair again. I know you can't hear me, but I really am sorry.'

Thus, eyes on the road, talking steadily, rehearsing aloud his plan, he drove her into Aylesbury. It was twenty-five past four.

It was an hour later that Robbie laid his bow across his knees and relaxed, pleased with his scores at a hundred yards; with himself and his fitness.

Particularly pleased with his fitness when he surveyed the Hospital's recent arrivals. Not erect in their chairs, and confident, like him, but hunched and desperate. He shook his head at the thought of the battle that lay ahead of them.

Each would already have been given a target of maximum physical rehabilitation and mental readjustment; and each would already be despairing of ever attaining that target. Every one of them would be exhausted every moment of every day by the prodigious exertions demanded of them.

Yet none, he knew, would give up, or become fed up, or be allowed even to contemplate giving up or becoming fed up : because everyone at Stoke helped everyone else. The strong in their chairs dragged the weak. Old sweats urged on rookies. And the staff encouraged them all. Two hundred and fifty maimed bodies propelling themselves out of inertia into a new way of life.

'How're you doing, Robbie?'

Turning his head, he saw the Chief Physiotherapist.

'Fine thanks, Charlie.'

'You looked thoughtful.'

'Don't know what I was thinking about.' Now he surveyed the more athletic of his fellow Stokers, as they threw javelins, putt shots, drew bows and parried and thrust with épées. 'You work miracles, don't you, Charlie?'

The Chief Physiotherapist grinned. 'Remember the day, about six months after you got here, you said, "Charlie, I'm sick of all this," and I slapped you?'

'You might have let me finish before you slapped me.'

' "I want to throw something," you said.'

'And you said, "Right. Be at the back of the theatre at 1.45." And when I got there you handed me a javelin and I threw myself out of my chair! Whereupon you handed me an eight pound shot and told me to see if I could do any better with that.'

'You'd have got the world record this year if you hadn't been half-witted enough to skimp your training and bugger your neck.'

'Not skimping this afternoon, though, am I?'

'I should hope not.'

'Maybe. But I've left my brother alone at the cottage.'

'He's a big boy now.'

'Rang him about an hour ago, to apologize . . .'

'Fair enough then.'

'. . . But either the line was out of order or he was so cheesed off he didn't answer. Leaving him on his own like that : not very hospitable, was it?'

'First things first,' the Chief Physiotherapist pontificated. 'Oh, dear,' peering over Robbie's shoulder. 'Look who's coming.'

'Oh, no!' groaned Robbie, for whom escape was impossible. 'Charlie, stay and protect me.'

'Protect yourself,' hissed Charlie. 'If necessary, shoot 'em' – and abandoned him to his fate. Which took the form of an advancing, middle-aged woman, dressed like a tart, and her even older husband, dressed like a trendy pederast.

'Robert!' crowed Mrs Lipton. 'How lovely to see you.' It was typical of her that she called him Robert when everyone else called him Robbie. Her lips were too red, her

hair too yellow and her figure quite out of control. Not
that she hadn't lashed herself into every control devised :
her softly oozing too pink flesh had simply defied them all.

'Mrs Lipton,' Robbie greeted her, nodding coolly. 'Mr
Lipton.'

'My dear chap!' said Mr Lipton, whose tiny hips,
sheathed in maroon suede, supported a flabby overhang
of green satined paunch.

'You must come to dinner,' Mrs Lipton commanded.
'And christen our brand new pool. What are you doing
tonight?'

'My brother's with me.'

'Then bring him too : we've always wanted to meet
him.' Ever since she'd been crowned Miss Skegness, in the
early fifties, Mrs Lipton had always wanted to meet
people; and since Stanley had acquired his paunch and his
fortune, it had become her obsession. 'Ring him now and
ask him,' she instructed.

Accompanied by the Liptons, Robbie wheeled himself
to the hospital's public telephone and dialled his own
number. He allowed it to ring thirteen times before hang-
ing up. 'Line must be out of order,' he reported, 'he
doesn't answer.'

'Perhaps you got a wrong number?' suggested Mrs
Lipton.

So Robbie dialled again. And again there was no
answer. 'Sorry,' he said. 'Definitely out of order. Afraid
we'll have to postpone that dinner.'

'That's what you always say,' Mrs Lipton pouted.

'What's the time?' Robbie asked her.

Mrs Lipton examined her diamond-crusted watch. 'Half
past five exactly,' she reported.

'Oh Lord,' exclaimed Robbie. 'I'm late. Thank you for
asking me' – and sped towards his car.

*   *   *

At which moment Mark was re-entering the back room of the cottage, carrying a folded wheelchair, a floppy purple hat, a rug and a neck brace; but no longer wearing either the wig or the Iron Cross.

'Jesus,' he muttered, looking at the electric clock. Robbie had said he'd be home at six. And Robbie never arrived at 'about' the stipulated time: he arrived, invariably, on the dot. So there were thirty minutes in hand.

Characteristically, Mark spent the first of those thirty minutes planning how most efficiently to do what had to be done. Then moved with precision.

He took off Robbie's plimsolls and T shirt and his own jeans. Repacking his jeans, he put on the shirt and slacks in which he had arrived. The rug, horn rimmed polaroid glasses, neck brace, T shirt and plimsolls he returned to their proper places in Robbie's bedroom. The folded wheel chair he opened and, having wiped it thoroughly with the dishcloth and sprinkled it with dust from the Hoover, folded it, shook more dust over it and carried it into the garage. Taking off his gloves, he brushed them clean and tossed them on top of his suitcase. Switching on the vacuum cleaner, he removed the dust he had spilt round the wheel chair. Restoring the vacuum cleaner to its cupboard, he took the purple hat to the stainless steel sink, squirted lighter fluid over it, set fire to it and carried it, blazing, into the garden.

From which he returned at two minutes to six.

One final glance round the room and, switching on the radio, he ruffled his hair and lay face down on the sofa, breathing deeply, as if asleep.

As the hands of the clock became vertical, he heard Robbie's car turning out of the lane and into the garage.

WEDNESDAY: SIX O'CLOCK

Robbie lugged his folded wheel chair out on to the garage floor and opened it, so that he could lever himself into it. Using only his hands, arms and shoulders, he had to transfer his twelve stones from driver's seat to wheel-chair.

It was a manoeuvre that usually exhausted and exasperated him; but now, so curious was he about Mark's failure to answer his telephone calls, he accomplished it with ease. Wheeling himself impatiently round the front of his car and through the door that led into the hall, he swung right into the back room and, a hand on either wheel, halted, frowning.

Because Mark lay flat on his face asleep. And because the room reeked of perfume and the radio was screeching. Jerking himself to the fire-place, he switched off the radio: then, wheeling about, sniffing, stared at his brother. And amiably demanded: 'Little brother, what on earth have you been up to?'

Genuine alarm made it easier for Mark to simulate an abrupt awakening. 'Eh?' – looking bleary and uncomprehending, rolling on to his side to face his brother. 'What'd you say?'

'I said' – with mock severity – 'what on earth have you been up to? The place stinks of perfume.' He sniffed again. 'And petrol.'

'Oh that? I – I spilt some aftershave. On the carpet. And tried to rub it off with lighter fluid.'

Robbie peered at the carpet. 'You've made a nasty *clean* patch.'

'I was getting a book out of my case, and the bottle fell out, and the top came off, and later I found I'd read the bloody book anyway—'

'But you hate aftershave. And even if you didn't, why use one that smells – if you don't mind my saying so – like boarding-school custard?'

'A passenger gave it to me.'

'Then she was either very mean or very poor.'

'Both actually,' agreed Mark, his composure regained. 'Surprised you can still smell it, though. I can't.'

'I've got a nose like a bloodhound,' Robbie told him, wheeling restlessly. 'You been out?'

Tyre marks on the sodden lawn, thought Mark. Forgot about them. Has he seen them? Better cover up; just in case.

'Engine's been running rough,' he explained. 'Fiddled about with it and took her out for a run. Worse if anything. So I thought to hell with it.'

'Why?'

'I dunno.' Because he couldn't think of a reason. 'Does everyone have to have a reason for doing everything?'

'You always do.'

'Well, this time I didn't.'

Standing, looking at the clock, he switched on the radio. 'I guess I wanted a kip.' His manner was edgy.

'Take it easy,' Robbie urged, wheeling himself to the fire-place and switching the radio off again. 'I wasn't prying.'

'I want to hear the news,' Mark told him, sharply.

Robbie grimaced. 'Can't imagine why. There's been none for years.'

Another uncharacteristic reference to the irrelevance, for him, of something the fit found vital. But this time delivered lightly; and therefore to be disputed with levity.

'For me, on my bridge, there's always the danger of a third world war,' Mark parried, 'so I must know who's currently stalking my command.' And switched the radio on again.

From which the newscaster's voice announced : 'Two more Liberian tankers collided this afternoon off the Goodwin Sands, making a total of sixteen this month. . . .'

'Those bloody Liberians,' Mark grumbled. 'Now I know who's stalking me.'

'Both vessels,' advised the newscaster, with evident satisfaction, 'are sinking. . . .'

'Where *is* Liberia?' asked Robbie.

'From six beaches in the vicinity,' gloated the newscaster, 'come reports of a massive oil slick which will hit all of them before morning.'

'Africa, I think.'

'Really? I'd have thought somewhere in the Caribbean.'

'Meantime numerous vessels are out spraying detergent.' The newscaster cleared his throat. 'And here is a special newsflash. From Aylesbury' – and his inflexion made clear his near incredulity that anything special should ever have happened in Aylesbury – 'we have just been advised by the police of the murder of yet another hitch-hiker. The body of twenty-three-year-old Janine Talbot, of Kings Langley, was found less than an hour ago in the back row of the stalls of a local cinema.'

Robbie wheeled himself to the refrigerator and poured himself a glass of milk, clearly bored by the violent world of the non-disabled; but the newscaster's voice continued implacably.

'The girl's mother, forty-five-year-old Mrs Mavis Talbot, a chicken sexer, told the police a few minutes ago that

Janine left home shortly after two this afternoon with the intention of hitch hiking to Aston Clinton to see her unemployed boy friend. The police say they are confident that she is the fourth victim, in just over a year, of the murderer now known as the Motorway Maniac. They point out that once again the victim was picked up on the A41, between the M1 turn off and Aylesbury; that once again the victim is a blonde in her middle twenties; that once again the victim was stabbed under the breast bone and through the heart; that once again the victim was apparently neither robbed nor sexually assaulted; and that once again the murderer has contrived to deposit his victim in a public place without attracting attention.

' "The murderer," says Detective Chief Superintendent Cheadle, who has headed the squad hunting the Motorway Maniac since his first brutal crime fourteen months ago, "is a man who hates young women and will murder again and again unless he is apprehended." He has asked us to emphasise that by now someone must suspect the identity of this dangerous man, and yet be protecting him.'

'Must we listen to this drivel?' protested Robbie, rolling back to the fire-place.

The newscaster became more cheerful, adopting the tone he usually reserved for Royal achievements on horseback and coups d'état in emergent Africa.

'The police do, however, have a positive lead at last,' he said. 'They are anxious to contact a young man, about five feet ten inches tall, strongly built and sun tanned, who has long fair hair, is wearing dark glasses, jeans, a T shirt and tennis shoes, and who was seen entering the Rex Cinema, Aylesbury, this afternoon at about four thirty. This man, or anyone knowing him, or his whereabouts, is asked to contact the Aylesbury Police. An early arrest, says Chief Superintendent Cheadle, is expected.'

Robbie switched off the radio contemptuously. 'I'm

sorry, Mark, but if you want the rest of your so-called news, get it in your car. An early arrest! What've they got on him now that they didn't have when he dumped the others outside those copper-shops?'

'According to that,' tapping the silent radio, 'someone who can help them with their enquiries.'

'Don't they always? And does he ever come forward? Be mad if he did, of course : they'd charge him as soon as they saw him.'

'Also, according to that,' staring at the radio, 'someone's protecting him.'

Robbie looked hard at his brother's averted head. 'And why,' he demanded, 'would anyone do that?'

Glancing down at him, Mark asked : 'Wouldn't you protect me?'

'You mean, if I knew *you* were this maniac? It's a hypothetical question and the hypothesis is absurd. Even if you did. . . .'

Frowning, he fell silent.

'Did what?' asked Mark.

Robbie headed for the kitchen. 'Time we ate. I'm starving.'

'Did what, Robbie?'

'Nothing.'

'Robbie! Did *what*?' – slapping the chinmey-piece with an open palm.

'Tell me you picked up a blonde nympho and that the last ten miles were "deadly".'

Mark allowed himself to collapse into an arm-chair. 'You know,' he confessed, 'you had me worried? For a minute, I thought you really did suspect me.'

'You?' snorted Robbie. 'A murderer? You can't even lie. You can't steal, you can't cheat and you're so guileless it's pathetic. You honestly thought I suspected you?'

'Well, I did say "deadly" : was a bit of a coincidence.'

'Should be a law against it,' Robbie agreed. 'But if ever you're involved in a murder, it'll be as the victim, not the killer, I promise you.'

Mark flushed. 'Just as well I was here all afternoon, though, isn't it? Not that I could prove it if I was asked to, mind you.'

'And why would anyone ask you to?'

'I came by the A41 : at the time they say the girl was on it.'

'So did a hundred others; and the bloke they're looking for has long fair hair. But if you *were* asked to prove you'd been here all afternoon, I'd swear I'd spent it with you.'

'And you say I can't lie,' scoffed Mark. 'How many people saw you practising at Stoke between four and half past five?'

'All right,' declared Robbie, unabashed. 'I'd say I telephoned you here at four thirty, and again just before five thirty, and spoke to you both times.'

'Why?'

'Because I'm not having you involved in a murder on account of a stupid coincidence.'

Mark shook his head. 'Why would you have *phoned* me?'

'To suggest you came down and joined me 'cos I'd decided you wouldn't put me off after all. How's that?'

'Very good. And the second time?'

'What second time?'

'Why'd you ring me the second time?'

'To ask if you'd like to dine with that awful Stanley Lipton and his even awfuller wife.'

'And how would you convince *them* of that?'

'Wouldn't have to : they did invite you.'

'They don't even know me.'

'Well, actually they invited me and I used you as an excuse. But, persistent as only the nouveau riche can be, they said bring him too – and made me ring you then and there.'

'So you did ring me?'

'Twice, like I said. To suggest you come to Stoke; and to ask if you wanted to dine with the awful Liptons. But the line was out of order, so the first time I couldn't, and the second time I happily told the Liptons *we* couldn't. The phone *didn't* ring, did it?'

'Not that I heard.' He hesitated. 'Seems I'm in the clear then?' Watching his brother closely.

'Just leave it to Robbie, you'll always be clear of the Liptons.'

'I meant, of suspicion.'

'Well, of course you are, you half wit.' But also hesitated. 'So long as no one saw you.'

'Saw me what?'

'Pick up the nympho. Did anyone?' – leaning forward in his chair, gripping the arm rests tightly.

'No.'

'You sure?'

'Yes.'

'Good!' Robbie relaxed and smiled, apparently oblivious of Mark's wariness. Yet apparently not as confident as he sounded : because almost at once he asked : 'Anyone see you put her down?'

'Well, I suppose so,' Mark answered fretfully. 'It *was* in front of the Post Office. Shouldn't think anyone really noticed, though. I mean, people don't, do they?'

'Who cares anyway? If no one knows you picked a girl up, why should the police want proof that you ever put her down?'

'Must you keep saying that?'

'Saying what?'

' "Put her down." You make her sound like a rabid dog.'

Robbie pondered the point. 'Gives one to think, doesn't it? The most innocent words. . . .' He lapsed into silence.

'You've lost me.'

'Traps.'

'I'm still lost.'

'Innocent words can be traps. "Deadly", you said. Sounds innocent enough. Until a blonde's found murdered. Anyone see you put her down?, I asked. Sounds innocent enough. Until someone who's picked up a blonde can't prove what he did with her.'

'Except,' Mark corrected, 'you *should* have said "set" her down.' Making it sound like an accusation.

To which Robbie blandly responded : 'You know you're right?'

'A Freudian slip?' Mark accused again.

'Meaning do I subconsciously think that you, little brother, are the much publicized Motorway Maniac? I've told you' – shaking his head – 'You couldn't be. That Scotch still on offer?'

'If you want it.'

'I want it.'

'Then I'll get it.'

Placidly Robbie watched him leave; but, as soon as he was alone, wheeled himself urgently to the carpet between the sofa and the fire-place and, gripping his arm-rests, leant forward to examine the clean spot. Releasing one hand, he even bent down to probe with a suspicious finger-tip : at which, straightening, he sniffed, his eyes meantime flickering up and down the sofa. Then turned to face the garden door; and sat motionless until Mark returned.

'Just a small one,' he instructed.

Mark poured deliberately and offered the glass. 'That do?'

He had delayed his return long enough to compose himself – and to remind himself of his duty to a disabled brother. A few moments ago he had felt close to violence. It must not happen again.

'Perfect,' said Robbie, waiting until Mark had poured a second drink. 'Cheers.' He sipped appreciatively. 'Know what I'd like to do tonight?'

'Scrabble?' Mark suggested. Robbie shook his head. 'Chess?' Robbie shook his head. 'Two handed bridge?'

'The flicks.'

'Anything good on locally?' The ease and amiability with which he asked the question surprised him.

'Only that Fellini thing at the Rex.'

'Seen it,' Mark told him, still apparently at ease; but no longer amiable.

'Really?' Robbie looked surprised. 'When?'

'Last voyage.' And thought, drop it, Robbie, drop it.

'Blast,' grumbled Robbie. 'The Rex is the only cinema I can get the chair into. Oh well. . . .' And Mark knew then that he had to seem willing to visit the scene of that afternoon's crime.

His eyes never leaving Robbie's, he said : 'We'll go to the Fellini thing' he could not bring himself to say 'to the Rex' – 'if you really want to.'

Robbie not only wanted to, he was clearly determined to. 'Sure you don't mind?' he asked.

'Why should I?' Mark bluffed. 'It's a super film : and I missed most of it last time.'

'Preoccupied with the bird beside you?' Robbie suggested slyly.

'Something like that.' Mark had the feeling they were playing Russian Roulette; five words out of every six being loaded. Or was it just his imagination; and were Robbie's double entendres as innocent as Robbie seemed to believe?

There was only one safe course : to resume the routine

of two brothers enjoying a few days together in the country and to avoid all but the most trivial topics of conversation.

'Time to eat,' he told Robbie. 'Don't argue : just go and wash your grubby face while I vulcanise our steaks.'

'Yes sir. Oh shit !'

'What's wrong?' – opening the refrigerator.

'I forgot to buy any vegetables.'

'There's a lettuce here. And some ropey looking tomatoes. I'll make a salad.'

'Dear old Mark,' grinned Robbie, heading for the bath-room, 'what'd I do without you? Come to that' – from the bathroom – 'what'd I do to deserve you?'

Exit Robbie, lobbing a last grenade, thought Mark – beginning to despair.

WEDNESDAY: SEVEN THIRTY

But the meal passed smoothly, Robbie regaling his brother with the latest local gossip – for which he had a sharp eye, an acute ear and an amusingly acid tongue.

'I feel a bit mean about the Liptons,' he confessed, however, as he dried the dishes Mark had washed. 'She and Stanley've done a lot for Stokers. And why shouldn't she be proud of her dirty big house and her vulgar new pool? Ten years ago Stanley was manager of an almost defunct cinema and she was his usherette: today he's a millionaire.'

'How come?'

'Strip clubs. Started with one: now he's got twelve. All highly moral. Look but don't touch! Our Stanley's a good Methodist. "There's nothing ob-seen," he always says, "about the body of a beautiful woman. Eve herself went naked, the Good Book says." Goes to church every Sunday and gives thousands to all our teams. That bow I've got, he bought me.'

'Sounds a good bloke.'

'He is. But I can't stand him. And Rose is all right too. No kids of her own, so she mothers us. Can't stand her, though, either. Reminds me of one of those great over-blown tropical flowers full of dead flies. All unzipped!'

'Robbie!'

'I know. When I got myself up to eight stone, but still

43

wanted to die because the physiotherapist had started me exercising with a bow I couldn't draw, Rose oozed alongside one afternoon and said, "You be a good boy and put on another three stone, Robert, and I'll make my Stanley give you the best bow money can buy". From that day on I never looked back. And the very day I hit eleven stone, Rose and Stanley arrived with my bow! Same story with dozens of us; and none of us can stand her. That the last?' – putting away a frying pan.

'That's it.'

'For someone who's looked after hand and foot at sea, you're very domesticated.'

'How's about we get the cousins along tomorrow for an evening's bridge?'

'Long as I play against you.'

'Against?' They usually played together.

'I enjoy squeezing. Margaret and Andrew haven't a clue about discards. No fun squeezing them. Hey, it's twenty to eight.'

They left in Robbie's car – Robbie driving – and spent most of the trip into Aylesbury discussing the relative merits of the strong and weak no trump opening bid.

'Well, for someone like you,' Mark concluded, as they approached the Rex, 'the strong no trump's all right 'cos you always hold all the cards; but if ever I'm lucky enough to get twleve points, I want to open.'

'Much better sit quiet and let me get into trouble,' Robbie counselled. 'Hell' – glancing sideways as they passed the Rex. 'Place is swarming with cops!'

'There *has* been a murder.'

'Four hours ago,' Robbie cavilled, swinging into the parking lot. 'What do they think they'll find? The murderer returned to the scene of his crime?'

Mark made no effort to answer: just got out of the car and waited, back turned, till Robbie had laboured into

his chair. Together then – Robbie controlling his wheels
on the downward slope, Mark walking briskly beside him –
they approached the Rex.

A tall, crumple-suited, middle-aged man, his grey hair
combed so sleekly back he looked as if he'd been swim-
ming in glycerine, waved them officiously away from the
foyer. Into which Robbie promptly wheeled himself.

'Are you blind?' the man snarled.

'Just crippled,' retorted Robbie. 'How about you?'

'I,' the man pronounced, 'am a police officer heading
an investigation into a murder.'

Chief Superintendent Cheadle, thought Mark, remembering the newscast.

'Good for you,' congratulated Robbie. 'What time's the
film start?'

'This cinema, sir, is closed.'

'You seem to persist in your assumption that because
I'm in a wheelchair, I'm blind. Wheelchairs,' Robbie
explained, 'are for the disabled. The blind carry sticks.'

'That'll do,' rumbled the Chief Superintendent.

'As one of the blessedly sighted,' Robbie continued,
undaunted, 'I am, of course, aware that this cinema, for
the moment, is closed; but what I asked you was, when
will it re-open? In other words' – gazing sardonically
round – 'when will this chaos of coppers, this frenzy of
fuzz, this perplexity of pigs disperse, so that law abiding
citizens like myself may enjoy the creative art of Mr
Fellini?'

'I've no idea,' rasped the Chief Superintendent.

'In that case, constable,' commanded Robbie regally,
'pray take me to someone who has.'

'Sergeant!' bellowed the Chief Superintendent. A blank-
faced, fair haired six footer in cavalry twill slacks and the
inevitable checked jacket materialised beside him.

'Now,' the Chief Superintendent advised, 'you will give

my sergeant your name and address and you will then
move along. Where, I don't care – though I would prefer it
to be one of the colonies – but either you'll move along or
I'll arrest you : for obstructing the police in the prosecution
of their duties.'

'Is that what this shower's supposed to be—?'

'Your name and address, sir!' roared the Chief
Superintendent.

'Lionel Barrymore, late of Hollywood,' Robbie recited
promptly.

'Give it to him, Robbie.' Mark had had enough. His
brother's almost frenetic flippancy terrified him.

'Robert Stephen Gifford,' sighed Robbie. 'The Wheel –
In—'

'*Wheel* – In?' Obviously the Chief Superintendent dis-
approved black humour.

'It's a joke,' Mark explained, anxious lest Cheadle take
even further umbrage.

'On the contrary,' disputed Robbie, 'it's perfectly serious
and very apt. Furthermore, it's painted in gothic letters on
a varnished piece of rather rustic oak affixed to my garden
gate.'

'WHEEL INN,' the Sergeant printed in his notebook.

'Wheel – In where, sir?' Cheadle enquired, with controlled fury.

'Brewers Lane. You go about three miles down this
road, turn left past the Mucky Duck, right just before St
Penelope's, and you can't miss it.'

'Aylesbury?'

'Thereabouts.'

'Aston Clinton,' Mark amended.

'*Thank* you, sir,' said Cheadle.

Mark squeezed his brother's shoulder, warning him that
he had gone far enough. 'I'll pick you up round the
corner,' he instructed. 'Good night, Chief Superintendent.'

'Good night, sir.'

'Goodnight, Sergeant.' But the Sergeant seemed not to
hear, so Mark strode back to the car park while Robbie
allowed his chair to roll smoothly away and round the
corner into the dim-lit side street flanking the cinema.
There, halting, he waited for Mark.

Who reversed up the side street a few minutes later and,
opening the driver's door by the pavement, sliding across
the front seat, sat silent as Robbie hauled first himself and
then his chair into the car.

Confidently manipulating his difficult hand controls,
Robbie pulled away from the kerb, up the hill, and headed
for home. For half a mile, neither spoke: then it was
Robbie who broke the silence. 'Bloody fiasco that was,'
he complained, his reaction to the police cordon apparently
nothing more than disappointment at missing a film.

'I suppose we should have known. . . .'

'Oh I *knew*. But that's no reason to close the place for
the bloody night.'

'A girl *has* been murdered,' Mark reminded once again.

Robbie swept the point aside. 'Girls are murdered,
babies suffocate, soldiers kill one another, young men become paraplegics – life goes on.'

'I'm sorry you didn't get to see your film.'

Intended only as a polite end to a disagreeable subject,
Mark realized that it sounded like sarcasm, and was re-
lieved to see that his brother took no offence. Instead,
Robbie gave him an apologetic grin.

'I'm being childish, aren't I? In a way, though, I am
childish. I get excited when you come down. Find myself thinking "Mark's coming. With stories of the big,
brave, outside world! And presents." I know' – raising a
hand that forestalled all protests – 'I know I say take your
whisky back to your scruffy mates; but really I look forward to getting it. And I even think, just like a kid,

maybe he'll take me out, to the flicks, anywhere, I don't care, so long as it's out, and I'm taken. Ridiculous, isn't it?'

'No,' Mark muttered, remembering how often he had forgotten to take Robbie out, glad to be able to sit at home and talk after his voyages round the world.

'It is, you know. For one thing, I'm five years older than you : for another, the last thing I can afford is to feel sorry for myself.'

'Wouldn't it be better', Mark wondered, 'if sometimes you did?'

'Better than what?'

'Bottling it up?' Tentatively.

'But I don't!' Robbie turned confidently into the narrow lane and Mark waited for him to continue. Quite deliberately, though, Robbie digressed. 'Can't get over all those swarming coppers. I mean, what do they think they were looking for?'

'Clues, I suppose.' He wasn't really listening. He was wondering just how much Robbie had provoked the Chief Superintendent. What damage had been done.

'One of their clues,' returned Robbie, 'being *my* name and address?'

'You did rather throw your weight about.'

'Never.'

'You called him constable.'

'So?'

'He's a chief superintendent.'

'I'll plead insanity!' Robbie decided, turning into his gateway and coasting into the garage, where he switched off the ignition. 'Or say I had a blackout—' watching his brother get despondently out of the car and close the garage door. 'My Lord, I'll say' – grunting as he dropped his chair by his open door – 'I'm sorry' – manoeuvring himself into the chair – 'but all I could see'

– breathing heavily – 'was this horrible face leering down and shouting at me.' He wheeled himself through the door into the hall, Mark standing aside to let him pass. 'Shouting, "When did you last see your brother?" And that's all I remember, my Lord. I must've had a blackout.'

As one of his physiotherapists had once remarked, Robbie was almost incorrigibly frivolous : which often made it almost impossible to understand him.

WEDNESDAY: FIVE PAST NINE

Mark had had a shower, Robbie had made a pot of tea, they had just finished their first cup and Mark, clad only in a thigh length, blue bathrobe, was setting up the camp bed on which he would sleep. Robbie's eyes followed his brother's every effortless movement, their greyness bleak as they surveyed the bare tanned legs beneath the short blue gown.

'You think I went too far, don't you?' he said at last.

Determined to avoid a clash, Mark looked up vaguely and said : 'Too far?'

'With the copper.'

Mark chose his words carefully. 'I don't think you exactly endeared yourself.'

'Should I have?' Robbie challenged, as if he wanted a clash.

'That's your business.'

'Only?' Still challenging.

'I dunno, Robbie. You made your point – that you don't really like coppers – so why rub their noses in it? Why not just have given them your name and address and left it at that?'

'I did.' The door bell rang. 'See who it is, will you?'

'You told them Lionel Barrymore, The Plucked Duck—'

'Mucky Duck.'

The bell rang again and Mark headed up the hall –
'And a non-existent church.'

'And that mute of a sergeant wrote it all down!'
shouted Robbie gleefully after him. 'But I did add "you
can't miss it", which in this country means you always
will, so I played fair, didn't I? Didn't I?' – listening.
'Mark, if that's Margaret or Andrew, bring 'em in.'

'It isn't Margaret or Andrew,' Mark reported from
behind him.

Robbie looked round. 'Oh, my gawd,' he groaned
'They've come for me already!'

'Detective Chief Superintendent Cheadle and Detective
Sergeant Robinson,' Mark introduced.

'I trust you found my directions helpful?' Robbie enquired.

'Well, actually, sir, I think my sergeant must have
misheard you,' Cheadle confessed.

The Sergeant looked blank.

'*Can* he hear?' asked Robbie.

'Oh yes, sir.' And stood, looking down at him. At
which, briefly, Robbie's blitheness deserted him.

'Superintendent,' he advised, 'even from behind I detest being gawped at. To my face, it's intolerable.'

Promptly averting his eyes, a discomfited Cheadle said :
'I'm sorry, sir.'

Robbie wheeled himself to the kitchen. Whence, hands
folded on his lap, elbows on arm-rests, deliberately changing mood, he announced : 'Well, whatever I'm supposed
to have done, I'm pleading blackouts and the Fifth Amend-
ment. Or does that only work in the United States?'

Cheadle smiled. 'I don't think it'd do you much good
at the Old Bailey, sir.'

'Oh dear!'

'But actually, Mr Gifford, it's nothing *you've* done I've
come about.' Robbie nodded graciously 'It's something I

did. I'm afraid I was rather rude to you.'

'I cried all the way home,' Robbie rebuked him.

'Poor Mr Gifford,' consoled Cheadle. 'And all I can say, by way of mitigation, is that I'd just rushed down from the Yard, everything had gone wrong and the Press were driving me mad. But when I realized we were passing this way, and that your lights were on—'

'You felt you simply had to drop in?' The way Robbie said it, it was so sweetly surprised as to be downright insulting; but Cheadle, it seemed, was impervious to insults.

Nodding eagerly, he said : 'To apologize, sir. The cinema manager told me you're quite a celebrity.'

'So's the Prime Minister,' reminded Robbie in his most cavalier fashion. 'But that doesn't mean that when I see the lights on at Number Ten I feel impelled to drop in to apologize for my chronic rudeness about his political ineptitude.'

'No, sir; but I need your help.'

'And we all need the Prime Minister's! However, since you now admit that it wasn't to apologize that you "dropped in", perhaps you'll be kind enough to tell me why you did?'

'Come off it, Robbie,' Mark growled.

'Well . . . closing cinemas unnecessarily and dropping in uninvited on anyone debauched enough to have lights on at ten past nine. I mean, he's *supposed* to be investigating *four* murders!'

'Mr Gifford,' Cheadle interposed, 'I believe you regularly visit all those in this county who, like yourself, are disabled and live away from the hospital at Stoke Mandeville?'

'I occasionally,' Robbie loftily corrected, 'visit some of them who aren't doing as well as they should.'

Cheadle, who was longing to sit, glanced at the sofa. The request was unmistakable. Just as unmistakably,

Robbie backed his chair into the space between the sofa and the nearest armchair, and blocked all access to both. 'Now I don't have to break my neck looking up at you,' he advised, smiling contentedly.

'Then at last we're all comfortable,' responded Cheadle, glancing gamely from Robbie, who sat erect in his chair, to Mark, who lounged barelegged against the back of the sofa, to his sergeant, who, notebook and ball point pen at the alert, stood motionless as something from Madame Tussaud's.

'You wanted my help,' prompted Robbie.

'Ah, yes, sir. As someone who occasionally visits some of this county's disabled who aren't doing as well as they should, how would you class a person who allows her wheelchair to be *pushed*?'

In spite of himself, Robbie was interested. 'A paraplegic?' he asked.

'Yes.'

'Pushed up hill?'

'No, sir; downhill.'

'Definitely not doing as well as she should. Who is she?'

'That's what I came to ask you, sir.' Cheadle was all deference.

'From this county, you said?' Robbie's antipathy seemed to have vanished.

'Yes.'

'No idea' – as antipathetic as ever, looking ostentatiously over his shoulder at the clock.

Cheadle ignored the hint. 'Her boy friend,' he elaborated, 'or possibly her brother, is good looking, of medium height, dresses hippy style, has long fair hair—'

'Is in his middle twenties and is wanted by you to help with your enquiries,' chanted Robbie. 'We heard it on the radio.'

Ah, that explains how your brother knew my name

when you and I had our little clash at the Rex.' Cheadle smiled appreciatively at Mark. 'Heard my appeal on the news, did you, sir?'

'Yes.'

'You must have a good memory for names. Or has this Motorway Maniac laddie caught your imagination?'

'Hardly aware of him till today.'

'Oh come now, Mr Gifford: no one in Britain's been unaware of the Motorway Maniac since Fleet Street decided to call him that early this year when he committed his second murder.'

'I never read newspapers: I'm a sailor.'

'Royal or Merchant?'

'Merchant. At sea we get daily bulletins. Who's on strike, who's at war, the latest currency crises; but no murders. And ashore I've got out of the habit.'

'Of murdering?' quipped Cheadle.

'Of buying papers' Mark corrected, showing his perfect teeth as he smiled professionally.

'What about television?'

'At sea?'

'Of course: silly of me.' He returned to Robbie. 'Now – where were we?'

'My brother was innocently at sea and you and I were discussing an unidentified paraplegic and her hippy boy friend, who, according to your statement on the B.B.C., can help you with your enquiries.'

'Ah yes. Well, let me give you a description of the disabled girl. She's young, blonde, slim, wears a floppy purple hat and is rather pretty.'

'In this county,' declared Robbie flatly, 'there's no such person.'

Which perplexed the Chief Superintendent. 'But she was *seen*, being wheeled into the Rex by her long haired boy friend.'

'I don't care if she was seen being wheeled into Buckingham Palace by Prince Philip: in Buckingham*shire*
there's no such person.'

Cheadle looked more perplexed than ever. 'Well, what
about the man?'

'What about him?'

'Could he be one of Stoke Mandeville Hospital's regular
visitors? Does his description ring a bell?'

'He could be; but it doesn't.'

'He's a Scot. Does that ring a bell?'

'Wearing tartan jeans, was he?'

Refusing to be provoked, Cheadle said : 'The girl at
the box remembers his accent.'

'Well, hurrah for her,' responded Robbie; 'but he still
doesn't ring a bell.' And again looked backwards at the
clock.

'Just one thing more, then,' sighed Cheadle, apparently
taking the hint at last – which he was not. Robbie relaxed.
'If the cinema *had* been open tonight, and if you and
your brother *had* seen the film, how would you personally
have left the Rex?'

'By the side door.'

'Not through the foyer? The way you'd gone in?'

'The aisle to the side exit slopes downwards, Mr
Cheadle. Which we paraplegics prefer. And the street
outside that exit is usually deserted. Which I invariably
prefer. Getting myself and my chair into my car is quite
a performance; and while I'm giving it, I prefer not to
have an audience. As I was obliged to inform you a
moment ago, I detest being gawped at.'

'Of course, sir.' Cheadle turned to Mark. 'And you,
sir? How would you have left the Rex?'

'Through the foyer.'

'You wouldn't have helped your brother through the
side door first?'

'My brother wouldn't have let me help him first, he's very independent, and anyway the important thing would have been to get the car round to him as quickly as possible, so that he didn't get cold.'

'We don't *feel* the cold, Mr Cheadle,' Robbie explained, as if lecturing to a half wit, 'but we are susceptible to it.'

Cheadle glanced at his sergeant. 'Well,' he said, 'I think that clears *that* up, don't you, Sergeant?' The sergeant looked as animated as a guardsman in a sentry box confronted by yet another American tourist.

'I don't think,' Robbie stage whispered, 'he's entirely with you. Come to that' – in his normal voice – 'neither am I. Clears up what?'

'Why no one front-of-house saw the girl being wheeled out of the Rex by her boy friend. And why the usherette swears she saw a girl in a floppy hat wheeling herself out the side exit, unaccompanied.'

'Then what,' exploded Robbie, 'were all those stupid questions for? Don't tell me you couldn't have worked it out for yourselves?'

'Afraid we couldn't and didn't, Mr Gifford,' Cheadle apologized. 'But primarily, of course, I came to you hoping you could identify either the lassie, or the laddie, or both.'

'And what good would that have done you?

'Quite a lot, I suspect. They sat at the end of the back row; and twenty minutes later, after they left, when the film ended and the lights came up, Janine Talbot was found dead in the middle of that row. We think one or both of them may have seen her murderer.'

'They left before the film *ended*?' Robbie enquired, apparently aghast.

'Having entered after it began,' Cheadle confirmed.

'Sounds like one hell of a film.' Robbie jerked his chair round to face his brother. 'Thought you said it was super? What you saw of it?'

Cheadle's sleek grey head turned slowly to Mark. 'You've seen *part* of this film already, sir?'

Hands in robe pockets, ankles crossed as he leant against the back of the sofa, Mark nodded. 'Last voyage. On the Canberra. Had to go on duty before it ended. The film, not the voyage.'

Cheadle smiled at the little joke. 'I see. Nice boat is she, the Canberra?'

Boat, thought Mark. 'Except for the passengers.'

'I sometimes feel the same,' Cheadle confessed, 'about my passengers. The public.' He turned to Robbie and smiled broadly. 'As you may have observed, Mr Gifford.' He returned to Mark. 'Been on her long? I see from your photograph on the mantelpiece you're an officer.'

'Two years. Second officer.'

'I envy you. Well' – straightening his back, no longer troubling to conceal his exhaustion because this time he had finished – 'we mustn't intrude any longer. Thank you for your co-operation, gentlemen: you've been most helpful.'

'I'm sorry to hear that,' said Robbie.

'I'll show you out,' Mark intervened.

For an angry moment the chief superintendent hesitated. Then, curtly, nodded. 'Thank you. Goodnight, Mr Gifford' – to Robbie.

'Goodnight' – almost cooing.

The sergeant pocketed his notebook and ball point pen and Mark ushered the two policemen into the hall.

'Should I have further need of his expert advice,' Cheadle murmured apprehensively to Mark, 'do you think your brother would mind so much if I called again?'

'Any time you see the lights on!' shouted Robbie, who had been straining to catch whatever last words the chief superintendent might utter.

WEDNESDAY: NINE FIFTY FIVE

From the front door Mark watched the policemen depart and their car vanish. Then quietly closed the door and stood thoughtfully a moment in the hall, needing once again to be alone. But Robbie had to be faced. Bare-footed, he padded down the hall to the back room.

'You must be tired,' he suggested, hoping Robbie would go to bed.

'On the contrary, I feel very alert.'

Mark made himself smile companionably as he sat side-ways in the farther of the two chairs, his legs across its arms, apparently at ease. At once Robbie moved his wheel-chair forward to confront his brother, frowning as he did so.

'You look like a sceptical Ironside,' Mark forced him-self to comment.

'I was thinking what an idiot that Cheadle was. *Brilliantine* in this day and age.'

'It was probably fashionable in his. Anyway, does an addiction to brilliantine make him an idiot?'

'Not being able to work out how that dead girl got into the back row of the Rex does.'

Mark resisted the impulse to drop his eyes. Kept out of his eyes all apprehension. Even contrived an air of interested bewilderment.

'Then I guess I'm an idiot too.'

'But you haven't been heading the hunt for the Motor-way Maniac for the past year, have you? And you don't have a supporting cast of thousands, do you? He has, though. Yet still he can't see that the dead girl must be the girl who was wheeled into the cinema by her alleged boy friend.'

Mark allowed his eyes at last to drop and rubbed at a purple scar on his brown knee. He needed time to answer. Needed also to learn exactly how much Robbie knew. But no longer dared appear too interested. 'Cheadle says the usherette saw that girl wheel herself out,' he objected.

'Oh Mark : you know the Rex.'

Indeed I do, he thought, as aware as Robbie that its usherette never ushed : simply tore in half the proffered tickets and sat where she was, knitting, while the Rex's patrons broke their legs in the dark. The aisle to the side exit was the one farthest from her.

'From where she sits,' Robbie continued, 'with the lights down, all she'd have seen was the back of a receding wheelchair and above it a floppy hat.'

'She still saw the girl who was wheeled in wheeling herself out.'

'Apparently saw : not still.'

'Meaning?'

'The person in the wheelchair *wasn't* the girl : it was the lad – wearing the girl's hat – after he'd ditched the girl – who was dead – in the middle of the back row.'

'You're saying he killed her while she sat beside him at the end of the back row; carried her along to the middle; shoved on her hat and steamed off without anyone so much as hearing or seeing a thing?'

'I'm saying,' retorted Robbie, 'she was dead when he wheeled her in.'

'Which no one noticed?'

'No one,' Robbie told him, with all the dogmatism of

experience, 'ever notices anything about anyone in a wheel-chair.'

'No one fails to notice blokes carting bodies up and down the back rows of cinemas though.'

'Not in that cinema : not on a Wednesday afternoon.'

Mark argued no further. To do so was not only point-less, it was to protest too much. He had chosen the Rex precisely because he had known that the wooden parti-tion dividing the back stalls from the rear corridor would screen him from the eyes of the knitting usherette; and because, on weekday afternoons, there were never more than half a dozen old-age pensioners in the audience, all of them sitting in the stalls nearest the screen.

'On a Wednesday afternoon, in the back row of the Rex,' Robbie advised, confirming the wisdom of his de-cision not to argue, 'you could safely strip off and indulge in necrophilia.'

Though Mark grimaced with distaste, Robbie was un-repentant. 'All I'm wondering is why he bothered.'

'She wasn't even touched,' Mark gritted. 'It said so on the news.'

'Bothered to take her into the Rex,' Robbie corrected mildly. 'Much simpler to have dumped her behind a hedgerow.'

Mark let that pass; but he had still to find out how much Robbie knew.

'Shouldn't you also be wondering what the bloke did with the wheelchair once he got outside? Presuming, of course, that it was the bloke who was in the wheelchair?'

'He sat there till there was no one round, stood up, folded his chair and quietly stole away,' Robbie explained impatiently. 'Got to admire him, really, haven't you? He's got guts. *And* he'll get away with it.'

Having ascertained that Robbie knew everything, Mark next needed to learn his brother's intentions. 'He may,' he agreed grimly, 'unless you enlighten the idiot police.'

'Am I likely to?'

Their eyes met: Mark's calculating, Robbie's quizzical.

'Don't you think you should?'

This time it was Robbie's eyes that dropped. 'In my position,' he murmured wryly, 'one doesn't go volunteering solutions to puzzles like this. It's likely' – looking up again, meeting Mark's eyes again – 'to vex the person involved. Who's then likely to ensure that one vexes him no further.'

Mark blinked at the cool logic of it. 'So you'll be holding your tongue?' he suggested.

'Certainly.'

Mark rose from his chair and, arms stretched along the chimneypiece, gazing down at his brother, asked: 'Do you *want* him to get away with it?'

Just for a second, doubt dulled Robbie's eyes and compressed his lips. But only for a second. Then, staring at the hem of his brother's brief robe, he said: 'You're indecently exposed,' and wheeled himself to the refrigerator. Whence he added curtly: 'But to be frank with you, I don't really care. Not one way or the other.' He poured himself a glass of milk. 'Want some?'

Mark shook his head and adjusted his offending gown. 'Four girls,' he reminded, 'have been murdered.'

'Ah,' said Robbie, as if now they were discussing a different subject entirely, 'but one doesn't know why, does one? I mean, do *you* know why?'

'I wish I did,' Mark asserted. 'But whatever the reason, it's still murder.'

'Of four girls,' agreed Robbie, 'all picked up on the same road. In spite of which' – sipping at his milk – 'other girls like the one you picked up this afternoon will continue to haunt the A41, and continue to thumb lifts from solitary men as if they were positively anxious to die. And if that's what they want,' smiling brightly, 'who's to be blamed if it happens?'

'You can be as dispassionate about it as that?'

'Having long been denied all passion, it's not difficult for me to be dispassionate.'

'And callous?'

'Now you're being subjective. We're supposed to be having a purely-objective discussion about the hypothetical fate of future female hitch-hikers on the A41. Let me put it another way—'

'Do!'

'If it were sex, rather than the death-wish, that obsessed these future female hitch-hikers, would either of us blame the man who obliged them?'

'That's no analogy, Robbie. This guy doesn't want sex.'

'Probably doesn't want to murder either. Which makes the analogy fair. Do you think all the men who oblige nymphos like yours *want* to have it off? Course they don't. They're put in a position where they can't avoid it.'

'And you're suggesting that this A41 guy can't avoid obliging blondes with a death-wish?'

'Something like that.'

'Why not just avoid the road they hang about on?'

'There you have me,' Robbie admitted. 'My knowledge of psychiatry's based on a few clinics. I attended in fifth year; and unfortunately none of the patients who then submitted themselves to the profound probings of myself and my fellow students was a Motorway Maniac.'

'Then *what* are you talking about?'

'How right you are,' Robbie agreed. 'Our first night together in nine weeks and, of all things, we're talking murder.'

Mark shook his head in frustration. 'That's not what I meant.'

'Well it's what I meant.'

'Okay. One last question. Do you honestly believe this man's more sinned against than sinning?'

'For what it's worth' – and his shrug clearly indicated that it was the question he considered worthless – 'I do. Satisfied?'

'It's food for thought,' Mark acknowledged curtly.

'But you're still hungry?' Robbie mocked.

Mocked, Mark realized, as he had not done since his own days of randy curiosity and teenage crises.

'You always were deep,' he complained, returning to his arm-chair.

'Deep? My father half murdered me : my mother took his side : a thing like that. . . . Your parents, of course, were marvellous. But I was never certain they wouldn't get tired of me : so I refrained from committing myself.'

'At the age of five?'

Robbie shrugged. 'Orphanages teach precocity. Then you came along.'

Mark looked incredulous. 'You weren't *jealous*?'

'I'd have wrung your neck if I'd thought I could get away with it. Until I realized we were getting equal treatment and what a nice kid you were.' He shook his head. 'Happy days.'

'Beyond recall?'

'Another world, kiddo.' He tapped the wheels of his chair. 'These are my frontiers now. Then . . . they lay beyond infinity.'

'Even then, though, for a while, something went wrong between us, didn't it?'

'You began to grow up,' Robbie explained. 'You were given a room of your own; brought friends home from school in the holidays; shared your room with them; got interested in girls. . . .'

Mark frowned. 'And you were jealous again?'

'Of course. In all my life, you'd been the only thing I was sure of. I'd always had your devotion. And when I came home from Medical School to find I'd lost it to your angelic chum, Dibbs Minor—

'You hadn't lost it.'

'Had to share it then – I found I hated it. But,' philosophically, 'I adjusted.'

No, Mark thought, it was the angelic Dibbs Minor you adjusted. And after him, Cousin Margaret, horse-mad Annabel and dopey Deborah.

'Why?' he asked : meaning Margaret and Annabel and Deborah. Meaning even Dibbs Minor.

And instantly Robbie understood. 'My natural parents had rejected me and my new parents merely adopted me : you were the only relative I believed in and I was not about to lose you, little brother, not to anyone.'

At which Mark forgave the long ago betrayals, forgot the long ago uncomprehending pain, and felt only remorse that he had never recognized his brother's insatiable need for possessions and security.

'You really are deep, aren't you?'

'Almost bottomless at times. Other times' – whimsical suddenly – 'weightless. Like an astronaut floating inside his little capsule' – lifting both arms from the rests on his chair – 'while the life he grew up with recedes farther and faster from him, until there's nothing to link him to his past except that devoted voice from Houston.'

'You feel weightless, sitting like that?'

'Without my arms to register sensation, yes, of course I feel weightless.'

'God.' It was an aspect of paraplegia that had never occurred to him, who was so aware of his body.

'Why God? I trust my little capsule; and' – nodding at Mark, his left hand gripping its armrest to prevent his body toppling – 'I have my devoted voice.'

'Oh, Robbie.'

'I didn't mean to depress you,' Robbie disclaimed. 'I just meant that you give me the incentive to whirl weightlessly on till splashdown. My strange relationship with you, and my ungentlemanly passion for winning, they're all that keep me going.'

'You've explained a lot,' Mark told him, looking almost lighthearted.

Robbie grinned. 'You understand me now, do you?'

'Beginning to.' Smiling back, as if they had somehow averted a disaster.

'Well – don't force it. To understand something as complex as a person, you need intuition as well as logic. Which is why your friend Cheadle'll never understand, and therefore never be able to arrest, or convict, his Motorway Maniac. He's entirely lacking in intuition.'

'Juries don't convict on intuition,' Mark objected, sober again; wary as ever; wondering why Robbie refused to leave well enough alone.

'No arrest,' Robbie rebutted, 'no jury.'

'You mean . . . no intuition, no arrest?' Robbie nodded. 'Why?'

Wheeling himself to the fire-place, Robbie picked up his chest expander. 'Sit down,' he invited. Mark sat, and Robbie stretched and released the expander without apparent effort half a dozen times. 'Cheadle wants to identify the long haired hippy, right?'

'Right.'

'And he has logic, right?'

'Presumably.'

'But no intuition?'

'If you say so.'

'Oh, I say so' – dropping the chest expander with a clatter and taking up a sabre – ' 'cos if he had it, he'd have made use of it; to explain away the usherette's statement that she saw a *girl* wheeling herself out of the Rex by the side exit.'

He tapped Mark lightly on the inside of his bare thigh with the blade of his sabre. 'After all, Cheadle wasn't in the Rex and the usherette was, so mere logic obliges him to accept that what she thought she saw she did in fact see. But I wasn't there either. Yet intuition tells me that actually the girl was slumped dead in the back row and that it was her escort' – tapping Mark's chest – 'the usherette saw steaming off in that chair! In other words, Cheadle thinks the Scots hippy's a mere witness; and not even coppers charge witnesses with murder; so. . . .'

'So you don't think this hippy'll be arrested?'

'Not even if they find out who he is,' pronounced Robbie.

'Does your intuition identify him?'

Robbie shook his head. "My logic identifies him."

'Tell me more,' Mark suggested.

'No,' Robbie declined. 'I'll give you the facts and you tell me.'

'Okay.'

Robbie marshalled his thoughts before speaking; and when he did speak it was in a characteristically forensic manner to which his brother replied as if he were being cross-examined. 'The lad we're looking for knows the geography and audience habits of the Rex, right?'

'Assuming that he was disposing of a corpse and was not just a witness – yes.'

'And he knows that people deliberately don't look at the face of anyone being pushed in a wheelchair, right?'

'Again assuming—'

'Let's assume it.'

'Yes.'

'He has acces to a wheelchair and owns a car, right?'

'Yes.'

'He's in his middle twenties, of good physique and medium height, right?'

'Yes.'

'He's resourceful' – flourishing his sabre.

'Obviously.'

'And quite an actor?'

'Why?'

'To wheel a dead girl up to a cinema as if she were alive, and buy tickets for the two of them at the box office, he'd have to be, wouldn't he?'

'I see what you mean.'

'And being a resourceful actor, knowing that the woman in the box office is going to remember him anyway, 'cos he's bought two of the only half dozen seats she's sold all afternoon, one of 'em for a very conspicuous dolly girl in a wheelchair, what would he do?'

'No idea'

'He'd ensure that she remembered a guy who looked and sounded nothing like his real self.'

'How?'

'By dressing uncharacteristically, adopting a convincing Scottish accent, putting on dark glasses and wearing a blonde wig. So,' and again he tapped Mark on the chest, 'who is he?'

'There's no point my trying to work it out,' Mark bluffed, 'because your basic assumption doesn't make sense. Assuming he had a body to dispose of, why wouldn't he just have dumped it in the nearest ditch. Or, as you yourself suggested, behind the nearest hedgerow?'

Robbie sighed. 'Okay. Let's prove my basic assumption. The Motorway Maniac murdered his fourth blonde today, right?'

'Right.'

'And she was found in the Rex, right?'

'Yes.'

'Daring, no?'

'Very.'

'Daring like the other three – who were dumped outside police stations, right?'

'Yes.'

'But each of *them* was dumped at night, when it was dark. At four in the afternoon, where else but in a cinema is there both darkness and a huge element of risk?'

Biting his lip, Mark admitted : 'Nowhere.'

'And who else but the disappearing girl in the wheel-chair can be the girl who was subsequently found dead?'

Mark was incapable of further resistance. 'No one.'

'Then who else but the Scots laddie could've put her there; and why else did he so recklessly put her *there,* and not, as you suggest, in the nearest ditch, except to *prove* that it was the work of the Motorway Maniac?'

In the long silence that followed, Mark found that his brain no longer worked.

'You know everything, don't you?' he said slowly.

'Except,' flicking Mark's scalp with the point of his sabre, 'where he got the wig.'

'Even why he did it?'

'We both know why he did it,' Robbie told him gently.

Again Mark tried to think. Posed the complex question clearly and told himself that there must be an answer. Even told himself that for once there was unlimited time in which to find the answer. But no answer came : only despair – because now that the truth was out, life could never be the same.

'What should he do next?' he asked dully.

'Nothing,' Robbie assured him. 'The police'll never work it out; and I'm sure you don't expect me to do it for them?'

'No, but I almost wish you would.'

Robbie's head shot up. '*You* won't do anything foolish, will you?'

'Like what?' Too weary to care.

Harshly, Robbie told him : 'Like spilling your guts to the law.'

Unable to meet his brother's implacable eyes, Mark abjectly shook his head. Satisfied, Robbie replaced the sabre by the fire-place. But seemed dissatisfied that Mark remained slumped in his chair, head in hands.

'Hey,' he ordered, demanding his brother's attention. Sullenly, Mark looked up. 'I know you hate yourself, but you mustn't! For my sake. What's done, kiddo, is done.'

Mark flew out of his chair to glower down at Robbie. 'And how often,' he shouted, 'will it be done again?' Robbie refused to be intimidated. 'That's up to you, isn't it? The telephone's there. A few seconds' careless talk to that ape from Scotland Yard, all your worries'll be over.'

As unexpectedly as he had erupted, Mark wilted. 'You know I can't.'

'Well, if you change your mind, I shan't try to stop you,' Robbie promised. 'I'll be having a bath.'

WEDNESDAY: TEN FORTY FIVE

Had Mark been tempted to ring Cheadle, it would have been to no avail: the chief superintendent was in the pub that Stoke Mandeville's paraplegics use as their local, talking to people in wheelchairs.

But getting nowhere. None of the Stokers remembered any ex-inmate resembling the girl who had wheeled herself out of the Rex. And all of them denied that any friend of a Stoker was a hippy.

Even so, Cheadle felt no compulsion to return to his desk. Every other lead was being explored by his subordinates. The dead girl's distraught boy friend was being questioned again. Randy Horn had been asked to make himself available for an interview. The newspapers had agreed to print an appeal for any girls hitch-hiking on the A.41 that afternoon to ring their local police station. Policemen all over the country had been warned to look out for a car carrying a girl in a floppy purple hat and driven by a long haired, good-looking, tanned young man. All the routine checks were either being made or had long since been completed. He was entitled to a quiet pint with these nice people.

Doubly entitled, really (buying himself and four of the nice people another quiet pint), because he'd got a lot done already. Far more than in any of the Maniac's three previous murders, the victims of which had all been dis-

covered too late for coverage even in the following morning's papers. And by midday – when the evening papers
had accorded him hundreds of column inches – the trail
had been cold and his appeals for co-operation had
sounded futile.

This afternoon the Maniac and Randy Horn between
them had given him his first break as far as using the
media was concerned. Randy Horn's photograph with the
girl's name on the front and her address on the back had
led the Aylesbury Police straight to Mrs Talbot, the chicken
sexer. Who hadn't seemed surprised that her daughter
had come to a sticky end; but had known at what time
Janine had left home, and for what purpose. And the
fact that Janine's body had been discovered and reported
to him at a quarter past five had enabled him to issue
to all radio and TV stations a combined statement and
appeal, in time for their evening newscasts.

On this score, he hoped the pathologist's report wouldn't
make a liar of him by establishing that the late Miss
Talbot *had* been sexually assaulted. Admittedly she didn't
look as if she had (she looked, in fact, the sort who'd
have been disappointed if she hadn't) but he'd merely
been guessing – and had added the detail to his statement
only because it was now a publicly accepted fact that
the Maniac was not interested in sex. Actually, he often
thought, it was one of the reasons the public considered
him maniacal.

He turned to one of the nice people, a girl in
her twenties. 'Long way to come for a drink, isn't
it?'

'It's only three-quarters of a mile.'

'Don't think I could manage three-quarters of a mile
in a wheelchair.'

'Well, actually,' she smiled, '*you* couldn't. But after a
while, one gets the muscles to do it.'

She had, she told him, been a drama student before the car accident that crippled her.

'You must miss the theatre,' he sympathized.

'Not really. I was a rotten actress. It's the concerts I miss most. Though four of us did get down to the Festival Hall last week. It's got a ramp for wheelchairs.'

'But how'd you get there?'

'One of the girls has a modified Triumph Herald. We went in that. Rather a hoot actually. When we stopped at the Festival Hall, by the ramp, a young policeman, gorgeous he was, came rushing up and said, "you can't park here", and Margot – it was her car – said, "We know that, so please will you get that chair off the roof?" And he said "Well will one of you ladies give me a hand: it looks pretty heavy." That was a hoot too. We manage them on our own! Anyway, Margot told him none of *us* could help him because our three chairs were in the boot. And do you know what he said?'

'What?' obliged Cheadle.

'He pushed his helmet back and said "Don't tell me there's four of you in there and not a leg among the lot?" ' She looked wistful. 'He really was gorgeous, that policeman.'

Then all the nice people left; and Cheadle, concerned for their safety, drove slowly behind them as their crazy convoy of chairs, the weak hooked fore and aft between the strong, rode cheerfully down the crown of the road because, as Shirley, the one time drama student had explained, it was a little difficult on the side, on account of the camber.

As the last of them rolled into the hospital, he accelerated toward his Aylesbury hotel, reflecting that if the blonde who'd been seen leaving the Rex *was* in fact an ex-Stoker, she'd be quite capable by now of having wheeled herself to Edinburgh.

WEDNESDAY: ELEVEN FIFTEEN

His bath completed, Robbie pulled out the plug and watched the unfelt water subside. When the last of it had gone, he dried himself carefully; and then, just as carefully, dried the inside of the tub, because getting out of a slippery bath was risky.

Sitting in the dry, empty tub, he dragged his legs into a yoga position, put a hand on each rim, raised himself, swung so that he could lower his buttocks on to the rim beside his chair (from which he had removed the arm nearest the bath) pulled a nightshirt over his head, pushed himself outwards – both hands raised, his lurching trunk momentarily without support – grabbed the far arm of his chair with one hand, the near side of the bath with the other, transferred his rump from the rim of the bath to the seat of his chair, lugged his useless legs out of the bath and dropped them on to the foot rest, replaced the arm of his chair, unlocked his wheels and rolled himself into the back room.

The effort and concentration of removing himself from his bath had almost exhausted him. Ahead lay the further exertion of getting himself out of his chair and into his bed. And two hours later – and every two hours after that – he must wake and turn himself.

Mark watched him fiddle with an alarm clock and, in spite of the horror that now lay between them, felt the

73

familiar tug of compassion. 'Your turns?' he asked.

Robbie nodded, smiling resignedly. 'Sometimes I think I'd prefer the sores.'

'Tired?'

'It's been a long day.'

'I'm sorry. Forget the alarm : I'll turn you tonight.'

'What?' – uncertainly – 'Wake every two hours?'

'I doubt I'll be sleeping.'

Robbie's uncertainty vanished. Politely firm, he responded : 'Well, that's your business; but turns are mine. And now, if you'll excuse me' – placing the clock on his lap and a hand on each wheel – 'it's past my bed time.'

There seemed no point in either wishing the other goodnight. Robbie simply wheeled himself off and Mark simply watched him go. And, alone again, reverted to the problem of how to control his crippled brother : or how, most mercifully, to kill him.

Can I control him? he asked himself; and shook his head.

So you've *got* to kill him, he told himself. To his dismay, aloud.

Had Robbie heard?

He switched on the radio. And began to prowl the room.

He picked up the sabre, and rejected it; an arrow, and rejected it; the bottle of phenobarbs, and rejected them. Then took them up again.

They were, of course, the answer, if Robbie's death was to look like suicide.

But how, mercifully, could one stuff a bottleful of phenobarbs down the throat of a reluctant man with two of the most powerful arms in Britain?

'You can't,' Mark told himself : once again, aloud. And flung himself on to the camp bed.

The music wasn't loud enough, the camp bed wasn't

long enough and the pillow was too high. He threw the pillow to the floor and lay face downwards.

Then propped himself up on his elbows and nodded sickly at the obviousness of it. Babies suffocated in them : why not a cripple? Not even suicide : accidental.

But a terrifying way to die.

Or was it?

He turned on his back, picked up the pillow, held it above his face, looking at it, exhaled . . . and slammed it over his mouth and nose, pressing it tight with both hands, counting the seconds.

Thirteen, fourteen, fifteen—

Must breathe. Air. No air. Only smell of kapok. Take it off. No – relax: he'll be asleep. Balls: he'll wake and fight. Red flashes. Roaring. Must breathe. Must—

Appalled, he threw off the pillow : to lie there, gasping, and groaning, 'Oh Robbie, Robbie,' while Robbie, who had come to complain about the radio, and seen instead an instantly recognizable rehearsal of his own execution, wheeled himself silently back to his bedroom.

Switching off the radio and the lights, Mark lay on his back, head on intertwined hands. But did not sleep. And when, two hours later, he heard the clangour of Robbie's alarm, he ran along the hall, to help his brother turn.

But Robbie had locked his door.

THURSDAY: TEN A.M.

Cheadle had been up since seven and at work since eight.

Janine Talbot's unemployed boy friend had been proven guiltless, though unfaithful, by his number two girl friend, with whom he had been in bed the day before between the hours of 1.30 p.m. and 2.45 p.m.

The back row of the stalls had revealed to the experts hundreds of fingerprints, none of them on the files.

Four girls had responded to the appeal that anyone hitch-hiking on the A.41 the afternoon before should come forward. Two of them were locals, who had seen nothing of value; the third was a London typist, who had enjoyed a harmless lift with a lorry driver; the fourth lived in Carlisle and had encountered two men with staring eyes and big cars on the A.41 between two thirty and three. Both had tried to strangle her. Unfortunately, however, she had no idea where the A.41 was or how she could have got back from it to Carlisle by three fifteen, at which time her doctor had prescribed for her a new and stronger brand of tranquilliser.

There remained only Randy Horn: who had insisted (on the advice of Sammy, his public relations adviser) on coming to Aylesbury to answer questions rather than allow Cheadle to visit him in his huge, secluded home at Virginia Water. Randy Horn was due at ten fifteen; and already half the photographers in England – tipped off by

76

Randy's P.R. – were waiting outside Cheadle's head-quarters.

Cheadle worked on – telephoning, delegating, super-vizing – and Randy arrived at eleven. Cheadle disliked him at sight.

'Man,' exclaimed Randy, 'those photographers are really wild. And me stoned out of me mind. Like, brandy, you know; not hash. Don't want to get busted again, do we?' Randy had been busted three times already and doubtless, Cheadle reflected, had every drug squad alsa-tian in the South of England converging on Aylesbury at this very moment; but that was none of his business. His business was murder.

'Mr Horn,' he said, 'I take it you know why we asked to see you?'

'Sure, man. The chick with me photo, and when last did I lay her, and where, like, was I yesterday afternoon, right?'

'Just where you were yesterday afternoon, please. When your local constable called, you told him you couldn't remember.'

'Yeah, well I'd just got up, hadn't I? And I was stoned, wasn't I? But I can remember now.'

'Doubtless all those photographers cleared your mind?'

'Yeah.'

'Then where were you?'

'Recording. For E.M.I. They'll tell you.'

'I'll ask them,' Cheadle promised, angry that anyone should use a murder enquiry to drum up publicity. 'Good-bye, Mr Horn.'

'That *all*?' Randy had clearly come hoping to be arrested.

'Unless you want my autograph,' Cheadle told him.

Randy left and the photographers, journalists and

TV reporters crowded round him. 'No comment,' he insisted. 'Not till I seen my lawyer.'

Good for a pic and a front page headline, he reflected as he drove off in his Jensen with the black windows. A good boy, that Sammy : a real good boy.

In his make-shift office, Cheadle was combing his sleek grey hair. For the photographers. So it definitely wasn't the boy friend and it unfortunately wasn't Horn. Not that he'd ever thought it was either; but it was best to be sure.

'Sergeant,' he called. His sergeant appeared. 'I think we should pressure our sailor laddie. He's had long enough to think things over. Let's re-arrange our calls so we can visit him this afternoon.'

THURSDAY: TWO THIRTY

For Robbie and Mark the morning and their lunch had passed in apparent amiability, each having decided to avoid both the subject of murder and, as far as possible, the other.

Mark had tuned and polished his car; Robbie had trained with his weights and chest expander. Mark had washed the breakfast dishes; Robbie had made his bed. Mark had telephoned his cousins to arrange an evening's bridge; Robbie had telephoned Stoke Mandeville to arrange an archery shoot. Mark, from time to time, had switched on the radio: Robbie, from time to time, had switched it off. But outwardly they had not clashed.

Their inner reactions, however, were almost irreconcilable.

For Mark the destruction of their relationship was shocking. For Robbie it was a fact. Like the paralysis of his legs and trunk. Something to be lived with. Something to which he seemed to have adapted overnight.

Distrust could no more be amputated from a relationship than legs and trunk from a head. So what use to worry? He had supported a dead trunk and legs for the last six years: he and Mark must support the corpse of their fraternal trust for the rest of their lives, relying on courtesy and good humour to make their task tolerable.

After lunch, Robbie had said: 'I must finish cleaning

the house.' But in such a way as to imply no carping re-
minder of Mark's premature arrival the day before.

'Can I help?' Mark had offered politely.

'No.'

'Mind if I go for a spin then? I've been mucking about
with the timing again. Best I check it on an open road.'

'Whatever your timing may be, you go and check it,
kiddo. I'll stick to something I understand. Like hoovering.'

So Mark had driven off and Robbie, towing the Hoover
behind him, having finished the rest of the cottage, was
cleaning the hall. He had just passed the telephone when
it rang.

'Blast!' he muttered; and speeding his chair the length
of the hall, Hoover still in tow, snatched open the front
door, shot through it, reversed on the path outside and
sped back to the clamorous phone.

Whose receiver he snatched up. 'Yes,' he shouted, his
Hoover still whining. 'Who? Just a moment.' He switched
off the cleaner. 'Sorry; who is it?'

'Richard Fairburn,' the receiver told him.

'Oh – hi, Doc. What can I do for you?'

'I've been going over my notes. How's your neck?'

'Fine.'

'You sure?'

'Well, of course I am. What made you think—?'

'Just checking.'

'Yeah, well some of your thicker patients might believe
that, but not this one.'

'Don't be so touchy. Simply making a friendly call.'

'You *never* make friendly calls. You're far too busy
with professional ones. So what prompts—?'

'I told you. I've been looking over your notes.'

'Look' – Robbie was furious, because he was alarmed –
'cut it out. Either tell me the truth or ... I know what
it is: Mark's with you, isn't he?' – wheeling about to

check that Mark hadn't in fact returned. The living-room was empty. 'Isn't he?'

Behind him Chief Superintendent Cheadle and the Sergeant appeared in the front doorway; and halted.

'He is not.' Fairburn assured him.

'Then he's been with you.'

'He telephoned me.'

'That's more like it.'

'And he tells me you're complaining of stiffness in the neck. Says you told him it's affected your shooting. He suggests – and I'm inclined to agree with him – you should come back to Stoke for a rest and a check up.'

'Quite unnecessary : I couldn't feel fitter.'

'Robbie, you've got lesions—'

'I know I've got lesions.'

'I still can't imagine how anyone as experienced in these things as you could have been mad enough—'

'To lift a television set off a table and on to my lap with the arms of my chair down. I know. Don't tell me. But the bloody thing had gone on the blink for the umteenth time and the engineer bloke had shown me how to fix it.'

'Have you been fixing it again, lately?'

'No, I haven't. Now is there anything else you want to know? You're holding up my housework.'

'Nothing else, Robbie.'

'Good. And goodbye.'

Slamming the receiver on to its cradle, he glowered at his telephone. Until the doorbell rang.

'May I come in?' Cheadle inquired.

Irritably Robbie turned his chair, and even more irritably looked up at the light. 'It's off!'

'Well, I did happen to be passing.'

'And thought you'd call in. Again! Well, come in if you're coming.' Sourly his grey eyes flickered over the impassive sergeant. 'Bring Charlie McCarthy with you.'

Closing the door behind them, the two policemen followed him down the hall and into the back room.

'Sorry to hear about your neck, sir.' Cheadle sympathized.

'Been eavesdropping, have you?'

'You were on the phone, I hardly liked to interrupt;
and I couldn't help hearing. All right now, is it?'

'My neck?'

'The TV, sir?' – his inquisitive eyes roaming.

'I got rid of it. More trouble than it was worth.'

'Got a good price, I hope?' Demanding an answer.

'I returned it to the people I *rented* it from,' Robbie
growled. 'And don't tell me you came all this way just
to discuss my viewing habits.'

'No, sir : actually I came to see your brother. But I
gather he's with your doctor?'

'Why don't you ask my doctor?'

Cheadle was as impervious to sarcasm, it seemed, as
he had been to insults. In fact, he appeared delighted by
it. 'That's a very sensible idea, sir. Now why didn't you
think of that, Sergeant?'

Not a muscle moved in the sergeant's face. Still a
guardsman. Very faintly aggrieved perhaps – as if a col-
league had fainted, or a Corgi bitten him – but a guardsman nevertheless.

'Chatty, isn't he?' Robbie sneered.

'He prefers to listen, Mr Gifford. Er – what's his name?'

'I've no idea,' said Robbie. 'What's your name,
Sergeant?'

'Your doctor's name,' Cheadle amended amiably.

'Why?'

Cheadle gave him an almost patronising smile. 'So that
I may contact him,' he explained, 'and enquire as to your
brother's whereabouts.'

'Fairburn,' Robbie admitted. 'Richard Fairburn.'

'Lives locally, does he?'

'Unlike your disabled girl who was seen leaving the Rex, yes. At the hospital.'

'Then we'll be on our way,' lied Cheadle, who made as if to move, then glanced at Robbie's chair. 'Remarkable how you can manoeuvre that thing. We saw you careen in and out of the door with your vacuum cleaner behind you. For a moment we wondered whether someone mightn't be trying to do you a mischief, didn't we, Sergeant?'

'The phone rang. If I'm hoovering the hall beyond the phone, that's the quickest way back to it.'

'Most ingenious.'

'I have to be.'

'Manage everything for yourself, do you?'

He seemed genuinely interested and only vaguely ingratiating; and, in spite of himself, Robbie felt his hostility fading. 'I do.'

'Using only your arms?'

'And my wheels.' Smiling modestly.

Cheadle looked apologetic. 'I'm being tactless : forgive me. I didn't mean to embarrass you.'

One arm pressed to his stomach, Robbie laughed. 'Chief Superintendent,' he insisted, 'nothing embarrasses me. And if I told you how I did *every*thing, you'd be the embarrassed one.'

'I don't think I quite understand, sir.'

'Not to put it too crudely then, nothing from here down,' Robbie drew a line across his chest, 'works. Except involuntarily. Which is *not* what one wants. So when one does want something down here' – gesturing vaguely – 'to work, one has to make it do so.'

Cheadle looked very embarrassed indeed. Yet was unable to resist a morbid curiosity. 'You mean—?' Then lost his nerve.

'I warned you,' Robbie crowed. 'Tell you what, I'll show you.'

'*Sir*,' protested Cheadle.

'Now, now. It's nothing like that. What a dirty old man you are. No – let's take something more delicate than the organ you had in mind : let's take the diaphragm. Which doesn't work. Know what that means?'

'No, sir.'

'Means I can't laugh or cough.'

'But you did,' Cheadle contradicted. 'A minute ago. Didn't he, Sergeant? Ha ha, you went, sir; didn't he, Sergeant?'

The guardsman looked uncomprehending : as if required by the adjutant to confirm that his colonel had farted. Aware that he was more likely to deliver a Shakespearean sonnet in Urdu than answer, Robbie ignored him. 'Know how I did it?' he asked. Cheadle shook a dubious head. 'I placed my right arm across my diaphragm, and pressed. Like this.' And laughed. 'Or again, like this.' And coughed.

'Mr Gifford,' said Cheadle respectfully. 'I dips me lid to you.'

'Just tricks of the trade, Chief Superintendent. Mind you, it's not as easy as it looks. We paraplegics are only a hundred per cent safe with both arms on our arm rests, or both hands on our wheels. We tend, you see, to topple.'

Cheadle frowned. 'You mean – if you were to take both arms off your arm rests, or both hands off your wheels, you'd be in danger of falling out of your chair?'

'In grave danger. Unless I was perfectly balanced. Head high' – demonstrating – 'and well back.'

'Then I'm not surprised you hurt your neck. Really, sir' – he sounded quite reproachful – 'both arm rests removed and reaching *forward* to lift a TV off a table on to your lap, I'm surprised you didn't kill yourself.'

'I knew what I was doing.'

'Maybe, sir. But you listen to me. In future, if you've got anything heavy to lift, you call the police.'

For an instant Robbie seemed dumbstruck : then, arm pumping at diaphragm, shouted with laughter.

'Call the police?' he choked, swaying wildly.

'Head back, Mr Gifford!' Cheadle implored. 'Head. . . . And hold *tight*, sir.' With difficulty, Robbie controlled his mirth and his body. 'Ooh, you did frighten me,' Cheadle scolded, running a nervous hand over his slicked back hair. 'You should be more careful, sir. And when I say call the police if you've anything heavy to lift, you mustn't think I'm joking.'

'I'm sure you aren't,' Robbie acknowledged, without a trace of warmth, furious with Cheadle for having flattered him into dropping his guard. Even more furious that Cheadle – his expression of concern suddenly replaced by one of complacency – knew that his guard had gone up again.

Cheadle looked at his watch. 'Oh dear : your brother won't be with Doctor Fairburn now, will he? I'm afraid I've been naughty, just standing about talking when there's so much to do. You should've reminded me, Sergeant.'

The adjutant was now admitting that it was he who had farted; and the guardsman was having no part of that either.

'Busy, are you?' Robbie mocked them.

'Oh yes, Mr Gifford. Very.'

'Doing what? Apart from gate crashing?'

'Same old thing, sir – asking questions. Fourteen months we've been at it, you know. Interviewed twenty-eight thousand people—'

'And got nowhere.' From outside came the sound of a

car door slamming. 'Know what I'd do in your place?'

'No, sir. What would you do?'

'I'd arrest all the hitch-hikers.'

Mark appeared at the garden door.

'I don't quite follow you, sir.'

'No victims,' propounded Robbie, 'no murders.'

'Ah – but the Maniac'd go unpunished, wouldn't he? And we can't have that, can we?'

'Why not, since it looks like we're going to anyway?' Robbie demanded. And before Cheadle could comment on this heresy, called out : 'Come in, Mark. I can't stand hoverers.'

'Chief Superintendent : Sergeant,' Mark acknowledged, entering the room.

'We were talking about poor Mr Cheadle's painstaking enquiries,' Robbie informed him. 'So far his squad has done twenty-eight million interviews—'

'Thousand,' Cheadle corrected.

'And although he's no idea who he's looking for, he's pressing on regardless.'

'Oh, but on the contrary, Mr Gifford,' murmured Cheadle, all geniality vanished, 'we know exactly who we're looking for, and exactly where to find him.'

Robbie's head rose slowly and his eyes challenged the chief superintendent's. 'You do?'

'Oh yes.' Meeting the challenge serenely.

'Then why no arrest?'

'Because first we must find out exactly how and why he committed all these murders. Motive, sir, that's what I'm looking for now. And evidence. No point my arresting the guilty man if I can't get him convicted, is there?'

'Not much, no. Pity you've got no witnesses.'

'If that were true, it would indeed be a pity. As it happens, however, it isn't. We have our witness. Or rather' – staring vaguely at the target – 'we know who that witness is. And we're confident that sooner or later he'll talk. If only for fear of what the murderer may do to him; because he's very close to the murderer, and the murderer knows that *he* knows everything. Talking of which, sir' – turning to Mark – 'I wonder could you spare me some of your valuable time?'

'I shouldn't think there's anything I can tell you,' Mark objected.

'Well, one never knows : you may have seen something as you drove down. No' – holding up his hand – 'don't answer that now. Just think about it. I've some phone calls to make, and a lot of paper work to do – tedious, but we can't buck the system, can we? – so shall we say, in an hour's time? Four o'clock?'

'Suit yourself.'

'Let's make it half past four then. That'll give Sergeant Robinson time for his afternoon cup of tea. Very partial to tea, aren't you, Sergeant?'

'If four would suit you better,' suggested Robbie, 'I've no doubt you could bully me into making him his cup of tea.' It was so abrupt a switch of mood that both Mark and Cheadle wondered what had prompted it; but Mark was in no position to enquire, and Cheadle decided that he didn't care anyway.

'I think not, thank you, Mr Gifford,' he declined. 'Not when we're on duty. Come on, Charlie!' – and departed via the garden door.

Mark strode to the open front door and peered at the two policemen. They were examining the lawn by his car. Then they left, and he returned to Robbie.

'They're on to us,' he reported.

'Yes,' said Robbie calmly, 'I believe they are. But this much I promise you, little brother : I'll never let them arrest you.'

THURSDAY: FOUR FIFTEEN

Cheadle, who had been talking to Doctor Fairburn, sighed as his car turned out of the hospital gates.

'Sorry about the tea break, Sergeant,' he apologized. 'But he did go on a bit, didn't he?' Sergeant Robinson, driving steadily, said nothing. 'I suppose we could take a few minutes off if you're completely dehydrated. Or should we see those shops? Suppose we should, really. Yes. Aylesbury as fast as you like. And then we'll hit the Giffords.'

As they sped towards Aylesbury he thought over all that Doctor Fairburn had told him in the course of an interview allegedly aimed at establishing the identity of the girl who had been wheeled into the Rex, but very quickly transformed into a chat about things in general, and then – slyly – about people in particular, and finally, almost accidentally, about Mark, the devoted brother and Robbie, Stoke Mandeville's star patient and imminent tetraplegic.

'Tetraplegic?' Cheadle has asked.

'One who has lost the use of four limbs compared with the paraplegic, who had lost the use of only two,' Fairburn had explained.

'Does he know it's coming?'

'Oh yes.'

'How soon'll it come?'

'Any time in the next few months. Most likely at night.

88

He'll just wake up one night and find he can't move a thing.'

'And then?'

'Might be a year. Mark, of course, wants him to come back here at once. Says he does too much, which is true : that it's bound to hasten the inevitable, which is also true.'

'And it all stems from those lesions?'

'That's right.'

'Has Mr Mark told you anything about his plans – when it happens?'

'Says he'll quit the sea, live with his brother.'

'And what sort of life will that be?'

'Hell for Mark. Worse for Robbie.'

Surprised he doesn't kill himself,' Cheadle muttered. 'He'd just be a head on top of a corpse.'

'Some manage marvellously,' Fairburn remonstrated. 'And happily.'

'I don't doubt it for a second,' Cheadle acknowledged. 'It's just that Mr Robert doesn't strike me as the type to make a happy tetraplegic.'

'You're right, of course,' admitted Fairburn.

'An expensive hell for Mr Mark and a demoralizing one for Mr Robert,' Cheadle ruminated. 'That about it, doctor?'

'That'll be it.'

Suddenly Cheadle wished he'd never met the Giffords.

THURSDAY: FIVE PAST FIVE

For the twentieth time, Mark looked at the clock. 'Half past four, they said. Where the hell are they?'

'Probably sitting outside in their car waiting for your first shrill cries of hysteria,' Robbie advised him.

Which was closer to the truth than he realized. One of Cheadle's experts was, in fact, out on the lawn, kneeling by Mark's car, carefully spooning out plaster of paris. But neither Robbie nor Mark knew that. Nevertheless, Mark had begun to pace the floor.

'Oh for God's sake,' Robbie exploded, anchored in his chair. 'Pull yourself together.'

Mark halted. 'Keep your contempt for the police, Robbie: I'm in no mood for it and you're too vulnerable for it. Anyway, you should be admiring me. As you said, I've got guts!'

'More than I thought, certainly,' Robbie conceded.

'And while I'm at it – that Chief Superintendent's not the fool you think him.'

'He's no genius, either.'

'Genius enough to have got you talking.'

'About what?'

'I wish I knew. When I came in, though, you were relaxed, and you were talking. And neither of us can afford to be the one or do the other.' Robbie's wildly veering moods had frightened him.

Robbie looked sulky. 'I know what I'm doing.'

'I'm still asking you to treat that man with respect.'

'Respect a *copper*?' A Jew asked to respect Hitler could hardly have looked more outraged. 'Don't you know what happened when I broke my back?'

'I know your father slung you on to the edge of a table : what's that to do with coppers?'

The doorbell rang.

'I'll tell you later. And meantime I'll tell our genius of a Chief Superintendent absolutely nothing he doesn't already know, so stop your worrying.' He gave Mark an encouraging grin. 'Go on, let them in.'

Having admitted the two policemen, Mark led them down the hall, where Cheadle greeted Robbie politely. 'Good evening, sir. Sorry we're late.'

'Late are you? We hadn't noticed. Charlie enjoy his tea?'

'There was so much to do, I'm afraid he missed it.'

'Ah, how sad' – wheeling himself to the kitchen. 'And now we can't even offer him one because he's back on duty.'

Filling the kettle, he switched it on.

'May we sit, sir?'

'Do.'

Cheadle ensconced himself comfortably on the sofa, sideways, so that he could look back at Robbie. The sergeant sat upright in an armchair, eyes front, so that he could avoid looking at anyone.

'If your boot's on my sofa,' Robbie admonished, 'as it must be, remove it!'

Cheadle replaced the offending, highly polished shoe on the floor. From which he raised his eyes to ask : 'Been cleaning your carpet, Mr Gifford?'

Forestalling Robbie, Mark said : 'I spilt some after-shave.' And took the chair opposite the sergeant.

Cheadle beamed at him. 'On yourself as well as the carpet, I think?'

Mark frowned, wondering whether Robbie had been the chief superintendent's informant.

'My sergeant smelt it when we had yesterday evening's little contretemps outside the Rex, didn't you, Sergeant? Said it smelt like—'

'Custard?' chimed in Robbie.

'Beg pardon, sir?'

'I said custard, constable. Noticed it myself as soon as I came in.'

'Came in, Mr Gifford?'

'From outside, Mr Cheadle.'

'Would that have been before or after you went to Stoke Mandeville to train, may I ask?'

Robbie hesitated, transparently debating the wisdom of lying. Then answered, with obvious truthfulness, 'After.' But hastened to add: 'He was given the stuff – by an ungrateful passenger!'

Lazily Cheadle turned back to Mark, who faced him with a kind of laconic courtesy. 'When exactly did you spill it, sir?'

Mark's expression was one of untroubled candour. 'Yesterday afternoon.'

'Just after you got here?'

'About half an hour after.'

'That would have been about . . . three thirty?'

'About three forty.'

'So you arrived here at about three?'

'At ten past, exactly.'

'And came by the A.41?'

'The M.1, then the A.41, yes.' Robbie handed him a cup of tea. 'Thanks, Robbie.'

'Visit Mr Robert regularly, do you, sir?'

'Every time he comes home,' Robbie intervened, wheel-

ing himself to sit beside his brother, a cup and saucer
balanced on his lap. From which he raised the cup to sip
maliciously. 'Good brew that, if I do say so myself. Yep,
every time he docks at Southampton, down he comes.
And all the time he's away, he writes. He's a bloody
saint.'

'I'm sure he looks forward to seeing you, sir. And you,
Mr Mark, you come straight here each time from your
boat, do you?'

'No, I go up to London first, and ring Robbie from
there.'

'You have digs in London?'

'I share a flat.'

'Mind giving me your address?

'11, Cornwall Crescent, S.W.5.'

Cheadle nodded, and waited till the sergeant had
written it down. 'So,' he continued, 'you leave your boat—'
Mark frowned. 'Something wrong, sir?'

'Ship!'

'Not boat? Now I never knew that. Did you know
that, Sergeant? Ship, eh? Well, well. So, leave your ship,
travel up to London and ring your brother?'

'He's away a lot.'

'At his various athletic contests, no doubt?'

'I'm the world's worst correspondent,' Robbie explained.
'Until he rings, I'm afraid he never knows what I might
be doing from one day to the next.'

Full of understanding, Cheadle nodded. 'My Sergeant
tells me,' switching to Robbie with an ingratiating smile,
'you hold the world record for the javelin and have won
gold medals at the Commonwealth Games for fencing
and archery.'

But Robbie was not to be ingratiated. Not again. 'Your
sergeant's been busy.'

'During his tea break.'

'No wonder he's thirsty.'

Again Cheadle switched tactics. To Mark he seemed to do it as often, and almost as senselessly, as Robbie switched moods. Doubtless, though, it was part of his technique.

'Can someone in your condition,' Cheadle taunted Robbie, 'really throw a javelin?'

'You bring me your police champion,' Robbie retaliated, 'put him in a wheelchair, let him throw against me, and I bet you a tenner I beat him by twenty feet.'

Cheadle shook his head. 'I think I'll save my tenner.' And reverted to Mark. 'So you come here at times that suit your brother?'

'I come here,' Mark answered deliberately, 'at times that suit us both.'

'And you arrived, on this occasion, at about three?'

'At three ten precisely: as I've already told you twice.' He began to understand some of Robbie's curtness. Cheadle's apparently ingenuous, apparently inconsequential questions positively invited it.

'So you have,' agreed Cheadle, who was beginning to understand the disciplined mind that lay behind Mark's professional smile. 'Yes. . . .' He seemed undecided. Then, confidently, attacked. 'Where were you between half past four and six, yesterday afternoon?'

'He was here,' Robbie announced.

But Cheadle ignored him. 'All the time, sir?'

More easily than he had thought possible Mark answered the question he had dreaded. 'I was having a kip.'

Cheadle watched the sergeant write it down: then resumed his interrogation. 'That would be after you'd spilt your lotion?'

'Yes.'

'What sort of lotion was it?'

'*Birds*,' said Robbie. 'They sell it at Tescos. Don't tell me you're going to buy some?'

Aware that Robbie had interrupted to give his brother time to think of the name of any cologne or lotion, Cheadle contrived not only to conceal his anger, he even looked amused.

'My sergeant took a fancy to it; didn't you, Sergeant?'

'Well, it takes all kinds,' mused Robbie. 'Mark, the Sergeant's kinky for custard. Give him what's left of yours.'

Now it was Mark's turn to conceal anger : because Robbie's apparent diversion had turned out to be an ambush.

'I threw it away,' he told Cheadle, and Robbie, defiantly.

'Poor Sergeant,' mocked Robbie. 'First no tea and now no aftershave.'

It was time, Cheadle decided, to put this Mr Robert politely but firmly in his place. 'I'm sorry you resent our presence, sir; but this *is* a difficult case.'

But Robbie was in no mood for rebukes. On the contrary, reverting to his most cavalier manner, he went openly on to the offensive. 'I'm sure it is, you ingratiating twit. As also I'm sure that your Sergeant's proclivity for perfumes that can only be described as poofy advances your enquiries not at all.'

Unflinching, the sergeant took down every word.

'Then perhaps,' Cheadle suggested, 'we should return to the matter in hand?'

'Undoubtedly', concurred Robbie, 'you should.'

Cheadle stared thoughtfully at Mark. 'You were saying, sir,' he reminded, 'that between the hours of four thirty and six, yesterday, you were having a kip?'

'I was.'

'The entire time?'

Fractionally, Mark hesitated; but not Robbie.

'Probably for longer. I left him on that sofa at about half past three; and later I woke him twice.'

This alibi Cheadle rejected with scorn. 'From the *hospital,* sir?'

'By telephone,' retorted Robbie. 'At half past four; and again at half past five.'

'May I ask what prompted these calls?'

'You may. The first was to suggest he joined me at the hospital because – as I explained at the time to our chief physiotherapist – I felt guilty about leaving him here on his own. And the second was to ask whether he'd agree to dine with a boring couple called the Liptons – who'd just waylaid me and were insisting I invite him.'

'That would be Mr and Mrs Stanley Lipton, would it?' Cheadle enquired.

'Oh God,' groaned Robbie, 'don't tell me she's your sister? She's at least a thousand.'

'No, sir, she's not my sister.'

'Your daughter?'

'Nothing like that, sir.' Though Robbie now had the bit between his teeth, Cheadle was his impervious self again – and secure in his saddle. 'The Liptons live on the A.41,' he explained, 'and when we questioned them, at the time of the third girl's murder, they were most helpful.'

At which, at last, Robbie looked contrite. 'I've been obstreperous, haven't I?'

'On the contrary,' Cheadle assured him, heartily, 'you've told us a great deal. And now, Mr Mark, I wonder whether you can recall seeing anyone pick up any girl on any of the following dates?' He took a notebook from his pocket and turned its pages. 'Yes, here we are. The afternoon of August the fourth, last year? ... The evenings of April the twenty-ninth and July the tenth this year? ... Or yesterday afternoon at about half past two?'

'I saw no one pick up anyone yesterday,' Mark answered firmly. 'The other dates, I don't even remember which part of the world I was in.'

'The other dates, sir,' Cheadle prompted, 'your boat – I beg your pardon, ship – was at Southampton and you were in *this* part of the world. We've checked with the P and O.'

'Then I may well have been on my way down here. But I honestly couldn't say.' And could not have looked more honest. Master Mark, Cheadle decided, was the type of officer captains would send to tell passengers there was no need to worry when the ship was sinking, the radio had blown up, the lifeboats had been smashed to pieces and World War III had started.

There was a silence while the sergeant wrote and the chief superintendent pondered. A silence surprisingly broken by Robbie.

'Is it important?'

'It could be helpful,' Cheadle admitted.

'Well' – co-operative at last – 'we can easily find out.' And wheeled himself to his desk, from which he took two diaries. 'What date last year did you say?'

'August the fourth,' said Cheadle.

Robbie flicked over the pages, found August the fourth, read his entry for that day, and looked up at Cheadle, demanding the next date.

'April the twenty-ninth this year,' Cheadle obliged. Robbie checked the second diary; and again looked up.

'And July the tenth,' said Cheadle.

Robbie closed his diaries and frowned at Mark from across the room. 'You came down each of those days. *Did* you see anyone picking up anyone else?'

And all that Mark could do was shake his head. Though

he showed none of it, he felt as lost and close to tears as he had that night in the Pacific when he'd read the cable saying *Mother died in her sleep this morning. Our thoughts are with you. Robbie and Dad.* Exactly as he had when he'd seen his father die – and Robbie, from his chair, had extended a compassionate hand.

Which now he had snatched away.

'May I see those diaries, sir?' he heard Cheadle ask; and, as in a trance, saw Robbie surrender them. Saw Cheadle open one and examine it. Heard Cheadle say – to him – 'I see that on the nights of April the twenty-ninth and July the tenth of this year, sir, you left here almost as soon as you arrived? To visit "the cousins", as Mr Robert describes them.'

He knew what Cheadle meant. That on each of those nights a dead girl had been dumped outside a police station.

'I usually drop in on them,' he admitted wearily. 'We grew up together.'

'Would they be Gifford cousins?' Cheadle sounded not unsympathetic : though one never knew with policemen.

'Yes.'

'But you, Mr Robert, never accompany your brother on these visits to the cousins you grew up with?'

'They visit me twice a week at least,' Robbie told him. 'They're very good about it; but that doesn't entitle me to impose on them any further. Also I try not to monopolize Mark. And anyway, I'm supposed to avoid late nights.'

'Late nights are bad for you?'

'For my various athletic contests, as you so snidely described them.' His goodwill had been short-lived. He was as co-operative now as a kicked adder; and Cheadle, as if tired of his venom, withdrew.

'Knowing which, Mr Mark, you wouldn't expect Mr

Robert to accompany you if you told him you proposed
visiting your cousin after, say, you'd had dinner?'

Mark knew that there was no escape : that it was point-
less even to struggle. Worse than pointless – undignified.
He nodded, passively.

And was surprised when Cheadle, instead of arresting
him, turned his attention back to Robbie. 'I gather you're
a man of independent means, Mr Robert?'

'Now why should you gather that?'

'This house; your specially modified Morris 1100;
your clothes; your sporting equipment—'

'Mark bought them. All of them.'

'That's very generous of you, Mr Mark.'

Suspecting a snare, Mark answered curtly : 'My father
left me his money on the understanding that I looked
after my brother.'

'Well, that you've most certainly done. In fact' – glancing round the room, from the solid furniture to the
elaborate kitchen – 'it seems your brother need only ask
and you give.'

'My brother,' Mark contradicted, sure now that Cheadle
was laying a snare, 'has never "asked" for a thing. Not
as a child, not as a man. I "give" because he *is* my brother;
and because his . . . his well-being is important to
me.'

'Then may I suggest that next time you give him a
television you make it a portable?'

'I told you,' cut in Robbie, furiously, 'I rented it. So
don't blame Mark. If you must know, I've had the devil's
own job stopping him getting me one of those miniature
colour jobs.'

'Delighted to hear it, sir,' said Cheadle, who wasn't,
because his snare had been sprung without catching a
thing. 'Very hypnotic, colour TV. You'd be up all night
and your javelin throwing'd go to pot. Oh – that re-

minds me. One thing about this last dead girl that's really got us foxed : where did the Scots laddie find the chair he used for wheeling her into the Rex?'

'*Dead* girl? You said she wheeled herself *out* of the Rex!' Robbie looked aggrieved : as if he had been deliberately misled.

'Yes, sir. But now we know she didn't.'

'Why?'

'Because she doesn't exist. You told us that! "There's no such disabled girl", you told us : which obliged us to deduce that, if she wasn't disabled, she might have been dead. And the post-mortem's confirmed it. She died about two thirty. From which we must further deduce that the long haired Scots laddie – if he *was* long haired – and Scots—'

'And not a lassie!'

'Exactly. That the long haired Scots laddie somehow laid hands on a wheelchair the more easily to transport the deceased from one place to another.'

'Are you seriously suggesting he spotted her thumbing a lift, offered her one in a wheel chair, bumped her off en route, pushed her fifteen miles into Aylesbury and deposited her in the Rex?'

'No, sir. She was picked up in a car and murdered almost as soon as she entered it, if the post-mortem's right about the time of her death. What we're suggesting is that she was subsequently *transferred* to a wheelchair. But where did the laddie get hold of that chair? that's what bothers us. Because, at that time of day, people who need wheelchairs are *in* them, aren't they? So he can hardly have borrowed one, can he?'

Robbie raised his eyes to heaven at such a lack of imagination and, full of truculence, demanded : 'Why not? Hospitals have wheelchairs; air lines have wheelchairs; British Rail has wheelchairs; and plenty of people who

are disabled have *two* wheelchairs, both of which they're
unlikely to be occupying at the same time.'

Cheadle looked suitably enlightened. And asked : 'Do
you have two wheelchairs, Mr Robert?'

'Have had for months. Ever since Mark bought me this
new one.'

'Then I wonder,' Cheadle begged, 'if you'd let us borrow
your old one?'

'Can't imagine what good it'll do you,' begrudged Robbie, wheeling himself toward the hall, 'but if you want to
waste your time—'

'Er – the sergeant will get it, sir. If you'll tell him
where it is.'

'In the garage, folded against the wall.' He pointed.
'Through that door.' The sergeant left them. 'But you're
wrong.'

'Wrong, sir?'

'A dead girl in a wheelchair – her head'd flop! Be
very noticeable.'

Cheadle nodded. 'That's what we thought. But according to the P.M.—'

'Don't tell me Downing Street's got in on the act?'

'Post-mortem, sir,' Cheadle corrected patiently, wondering how long his patience could endure. 'According to
the post-mortem, the Scots laddie stopped her head from
flopping by propping it up.'

'Propping it *up*?' Robbie looked outraged. 'What with,
for God's sake? A garden stake?'

'Some kind of brace, sir. I don't suppose you've one of
them too, have you?'

'Why should I?'

'Your lesion trouble? After you'd lifted your TV off
the—'

'All right' – testily – 'so I've got a brace.'

'Might we see it?' Cheadle wondered.

The sergeant returned, carrying Robbie's old, folded chair by its wheels.

'In my wardrobe,' Robbie advised the sergeant, sighing. 'Top shelf. The bedroom's the second door to the right.'

'Thank you, Mr Robert,' said Cheadle.

'Anything else you want? Like a pair of calipers, a chest expander, a kitchen sink?'

'Just a quick re-cap, if I may. You, Mr Mark, arrived here at ten past three yesterday, having come by the M.1 and the A.41?'

'Yes.' Blue eyes watchful, calculating.

'And remained here all afternoon?'

'Except,' Mark qualified, his wits returned, his optimism restored, 'for about five minutes when I drove up and down the lane, testing my engine. It'd been running rough and I'd mucked about with the timing.'

'Ah, now I'm glad you remembered that. Explains *two* of the *three* sets of tyre tracks made by your car that we saw on the lawn this afternoon. Perhaps now you could tell me about the third?'

'Took her out again today. Been mucking about with her some more this morning.'

'I see.' He seemed satisfied. 'And you, Mr Robert, between four and six, were either en route to, at, or on your way back from Stoke Mandeville?'

'I was.'

'And at both four thirty and five thirty, you telephoned your brother, here?'

'I did.'

'And spoke to him on each occasion?'

'That's right.'

'Then, for the moment, I shall trouble you no further.'

'Thank God for that.'

'Except you won't mind, will you, sir, if we take away

your old chair and neckbrace? We're planning a little experiment, using one of our woman officers.'

'Help yourself.'

'Very kind of you, sir. Come along, Sergeant. Time's running out.' He turned to Mark. 'You'll be here to-morrow, will you, Mr Gifford?'

'Until seven.'

'Excellent. Nice for Mr Robert to have you so long : you must have lots to talk about! May we let ourselves out? I'll return your belongings tomorrow, Mr Robert. Some time between five and seven.'

'As long as it's not tonight : we're playing bridge.'

'So your Cousin Margaret told me,' observed Cheadle brightly. 'Enjoy your game. I'll look forward to seeing you both tomorrow.'

THURSDAY: TWENTY TO SIX

Wheeling himself to the sink, washing his cup and saucer, Robbie said: 'I thought they'd never go.'

Mark sighed and rose from his chair.

'Robbie, what are you playing at?'

'Playing at?'

'Those diaries, the old chair. . . .'

'You said, "treat him with respect".'

'And you said you'd tell him absolutely nothing'—

'That he didn't already know,' qualified Robbie.

'Which most certainly included the dates of each of my visits here since August of last year.'

'Do you seriously believe,' Robbie asked him, 'he wouldn't have dug them up for himself?' He put his cup and saucer in the crockery drawer. 'By volunteering them, I've completely disarmed him.'

'Having first savagely provoked him? Having called *him* a twit and his Sergeant a poof, you calmly sit there and tell me you completely disarmed him? Having scoffed gallons of tea right under their parched noses, and as good as told Cheadle to get on with his job?'

'*He* as good as told me my world records were a farce!'

Mark threw up his hands. '*He* wasn't *trying* to be rude.'

'*He* doesn't have to.'

'And *you* didn't have to tell him that daft story about talking to me twice on the telephone.'

'I suppose you'd rather I'd told him you were out all afternoon? That you'd spent the time I was out disposing of an unwanted corpse?'

Mark's rage gave way to despair. It was useless arguing. With Robbie (whose ability to twist words and not answer the question made politicians seem models of candour) it always had been.

'But, Robbie, that's virtually what you did tell him. Now why?'

'Look,' said Robbie, 'I know you're in a bit of a fix—'

'A fix, he calls it,' his brother groaned.

'—but one of us had to keep his head. Cheadle wasn't talking idly when he asked me where you'd got hold of a chair, you know.'

'Where the *Scots laddie* got hold of a chair.'

'If,' reminded Robbie, 'he was Scots! Anyway, why shout at me? All I did was put into his mind, as possible suspects, hospital porters, air-line stewards and British Rail ticket collectors.'

'You put into his mind,' Mark quietly corrected, 'your chair and me.'

'But he already knew it was you. He told us he knew who the Maniac was, and who his witness was. And both you and I know he wasn't bluffing. But that doesn't mean we just wave a white flag. *We*'ve got to bluff. We've got to disarm him by volunteering information he'd never expect us to volunteer. Can't you see that?'

'I can't see anything any longer.'

'After all you've done for me, do you seriously believe I'd let him pin those murders on you?'

'I try not to.'

'That's better.' Then, sitting slightly straighter : 'I presume you wiped her fingerprints off the chair?'

Mark nodded.

'*Was* it my brace you used?'

'Yes.'

'Clean that too?'

Again Mark nodded. 'And burnt her hat.'

'What about the wig?'

'Hers. Before I left the Rex, I put it on her.'

'Then they'll never arrest you.'

'Well, they won't give me a peerage, that's for sure.'

'I never knew you aspired to a peerage!'

'Cut the wise cracks, Robbie.'

'Was only trying to snap you out of it.' Conscious, nevertheless, that he'd gone too far.

'Why?'

'Because, in an hour's time, Margaret and Andrew'll be here for bridge.'

'Cancel it.'

'And let Cheadle know we're worried?'

'I *am* worried.'

'Mark, he's found no witnesses, no murder weapon and no motive. Let him suspect all he likes, know all he likes, he'll never be able to arrest you. You'd only get off.'

Mark's tanned cheeks glistened with sudden tears. Brushing them irritably away, he shouted : 'But it can't go on.'

'What can't go on?'

'Girls getting killed.'

'We've agreed,' Robbie reminded, 'that that depends entirely on you.'

'Is that *all* you can say?' Frantically beseeching something more.

But Robbie wouldn't help him. 'What else is there to say?'

'That four girls are dead! And for all you seem to care, it could soon be five, or six . . .'

'Or seven, or eight, or nine,' agreed Robbie. 'But they'll all of 'em matter less than us.' He wheeled himself into the hall.

'Where're you going?' his brother demanded.

Robbie grinned. 'Don't ask embarrassing questions.' And vanished into the bathroom.

'Robbie?' Mark called.

'What?'

'Why don't you go to Cheadle? Put an end to it?'

'That's your prerogative,' Robbie called back; but Mark sensed there was more to come. And was right. 'Set up the table, will you? And get out the cards and scorers.'

Life, as Robbie had earlier remarked, must go on. For the moment, life was an evening's bridge.

THURSDAY: HALF PAST SIX

Cheadle sat at a telephone, the receiver to his ear, waiting
for an answer, fingers drumming.

'Ah, Mr Lipton?' he asked.

'Yes. Who's that?'

'Chief Superintendent Cheadle here.'

'Hel*lo*, Chief Superintendent. How are you?'

'Busy, I'm afraid : which is why I'm telephoning—'

'Something I can do . . . ?'

'We've got a lead. Afraid I can't explain the
details. . . .'

'I quite understand, Chief Superintendent.' Mr Lipton
was the sort of man who liked to use peoples' ranks and
titles; and the higher the rank or title, the more frequently
he liked to use it.

'. . . except that the suspect's alibi hangs on whether or
not the telephone lines to Aston Clinton, on Wednesday
evening, were, as he alleges, out of order,' Cheadle lied
glibly.

'Yes?' Mr Lipton sounded lost.

'You see, no one but the suspect in Aston Clinton
seems to have used his phone at exactly that time, so
we're having trouble checking his story, and our one hope
seems to be a Mr Robert Gifford—'

'Know him well. Grand chap.'

'Indeed he is. Well, Mr Gifford told us you'd been

108

kind enough to invite him and his brother to dinner on Wednesday evening—'

'That's right, Chief Superintendent.' Mr Lipton had found himself again. 'He rang his brother at Aston Clinton at exactly 5.30 by my wife's diamond watch; and the line *was* out of order.'

'Oh no,' groaned Cheadle, smiling happily.

'Have I given your suspect his alibi?' Mr Lipton asked anxiously.

'Afraid so, Mr Lipton. You're sure he said "out of order"; not "no answer"?'

'He said out of order, Chief Superintendent. Of that I'm sure.'

'Bang goes another good lead, then,' lamented Cheadle. 'But thank you for your co-operation.'

'Not at all, Chief Superintendent. Goodbye.'

Cheadle hung up.

'Same story as the Chief Physiotherapist,' he told his sergeant. 'Line allegedly out of order. Which it may have been; but definitely Master Robert did not disturb our sailor laddie's kip. Not at four thirty. Not at five thirty. Never spoke to him at all. Interesting.' He rubbed at the bristles on his chin. 'But insufficient.'

He took an envelope from his trousers pocket and read some notes listed on the back. 'Still, these should do it,' he said; and passed the envelope to Sergeant Robinson.

To some the list might have seemed cryptic. Certainly the sergeant, to whom, apparently, everything seemed cryptic, simply stood his ground – a guardsman ordered to storm a fortress single handed – and awaited more detailed instructions.

'I think,' instructed Cheadle, 'you'd better start at the bottom. Get the wheelchair and put our lassie in it. In plain clothes, with a red nose, black teeth and a bow in her hair!'

Nodding, the sergeant left to storm his castle: while Cheadle asked the telephone exchange to get him the Weather Wallah.

'Weather what?' the exchange girl demanded.

'Wallah,' he repeated.

'What's his number then?'

'No idea, Miss. That's why I'm soliciting your aid.'

'The geezer on the telly said tomorrow's going to be fine all day except when it rains.'

'I want yesterday's weather, Miss.'

'Yesterday,' she told him coldly, 'it rained all day except when it was fine. You a nutter or something?'

'No, Miss, I'm a Police Officer; and I'd be obliged if you'd spare me the small talk and get me the Weather Wallah. Try M for Meteorological Office , or A, for Air Ministry Roof, or even G if you like.'

'What's G stand for?' she asked suspiciously.

'Geezer on Telly.'

'I think you are a nutter,' she told him; but dialled a number for him, which answered almost at once.

'I want to know the rainfall in Aston Clinton yesterday,' he requested. 'Yes, Wednesday. . . . Yes, I'll hang on.'

For three minutes he hung on. Then: 'Seventy-five points, give or take a few? . . . Between two forty and three ten? . . . Thank you.'

Next he rang a subordinate at Scotland Yard. 'By tomorrow midday,' he ordered, 'I want the wording and details of the Will of the late Francis Robert Marcus Gifford, of Chichester. I particularly want to know how much he left. Somerset House it'll be, won't it? . . . Well, I leave it to you.'

Finally he rang Glasgow. 'What'd you find out?' he asked; and listened intently. Then: 'What'd *we* do? . . . I see. Where's he now? . . . Okay. Thanks for your help. Goodbye.'

Rising from his desk, he walked to the next room, where a self-conscious policewoman sat in Robbie's old wheelchair, her nose reddened with lipstick, her front teeth blackened with insulating tape and in her hair a ludicrous bow.

'What's your Christian name?' he asked her.

'Iris, sir.'

'If I have to talk to you,' he advised, 'I'll call you Iris and you'll call me Ted. All right?'

'Yes, sir.'

'Yes, Ted.'

'Yes, Ted, sir.'

'And sit erect. That's better. But head high, Iris : like you were trying to hide a double chin.' Oh Gawd, she's *got* a double chin! Thinks I'm sending her up. 'That's it. Now your feet together.... Yes. And your forearms along the armrests, your fingers wrapped downwards. *Down-*wards, Iris' – she may have two chins but she's got no bloody brains. Smile at her. Paternally he smiled. 'Down-wards, Iris, over the ends. Good! So off we go.'

For the next half hour he pushed her round Aylesbury; and observed that oncomers invariably looked at anything but Iris's eyecatching face.

'She could have had leprosy and a hole in her head,' he advised his sergeant when they returned. 'She could've been dead! No one would have noticed.'

He found another envelope. 'Seventy-five points in thirty minutes,' he read. 'Well, you can handle that one, Sergeant.' He glanced at his watch and then out the window. 'Plenty of light still; and it's only half past seven.'

THURSDAY: HALF PAST SEVEN

To Margaret and Andrew their Gifford cousins presented a relaxed, united front, Robbie seizing the initiative as soon as they arrived.

'Ho, ho, young Andrew,' he bantered, 'what mischief have you been up to?'

'Me?' squeaked Andrew, who was twenty-two, ginger haired and interested only in rock climbing.

'You!' accused Robbie. 'Police been here all afternoon: trying to break your alibis for when you murdered those three girls but said you were talking with Mark each time.'

'They think *I* did it?'

'Don't worry. I showed them my diary, which proved Mark *was* with you, and Mark confirmed it.'

'But they asked *me* about Mark.'

'They asked Mark about *me*.'

'The sods!'

Robbie gave his cousin the comforting smile acquired in his student days when he'd had to ask intimate questions of embarrassed patients. Had fate allowed him to qualify, it would have earned him a fortune. As it was, it placated Andrew. To whom he explained: 'Not to worry. They're only doing their job.' Which disposed of such disagreeable topics as multi-murder. 'How are you, sweet Meg?'

'A bit relieved, actually,' she confessed, blushing. 'That Superintendent Cheeseman or whoever he was—'

'Cheadle, my love.'

'We thought *he* thought Mark—'

'Mark? Never. No, old Cheadle's just lashing out in every conceivable direction on the principle that he can't go on missing his murderer for ever. He even had a go at Stanley.'

'At Mr Lipton?'

'At Mr Lipton no less.' Robbie assured her. 'Told me so himself. Said he'd questioned both Stanley and Rose at the time of the last murder and they'd been very helpful. Which is more than I was, I can tell you. However, enough of that. Andrew, shall we take them on?'

And for the next three hours they played bridge – Andrew cautiously, Mark skilfully, Margaret unimaginatively and Robbie brilliantly.

'Six diamonds,' he opened, on the final hand. He held seven winning diamonds, three winning hearts and three spades to the queen; and he knew, by the way Margaret frowned as she arranged her cards, that she had opening points. Margaret always frowned when she had opening points. Which, in this case, could only be the tops in clubs – of which he had none – and spades. So Margaret would double; and he would re-double; and Margaret, who always led her major suit first, would lead her ace of spades; and he would play his queen of spades; and Margaret (thinking, if she had the king, he had no more spades; if she hadn't the king, that he had it) would lead another suit – and he'd be home and dry.

Margaret doubled; he re-doubled; Margaret led her ace of spades; he put up his queen of spades; Margaret hesitated – and led the ace of clubs.

He took the trick with a small trump, cleared trumps with his ace and king, led the ace of hearts, and frowned before leading again. Margaret smiled, convinced that his weakness lay in hearts – of which she had four to the knave.

Sighing, as if defeat were inevitable, Robbie led out four diamonds in succession, and watched Margaret discard four spades to the king and the king of clubs. Then he led his king and queen of hearts. Which left two small spades in dummy and two even smaller spades in his own hand. One small slam, doubled, re-doubled, vulnerable – made.

Laying down his last two cards, he said : 'Sorry, Meg' – and, thumping his diaphragm, burst out laughing.

'Oh *Robbie*,' she protested, blushing again, 'How could you?' Smiling bravely, she left with Andrew ten minutes later.

'She's right, you know,' Mark reproached, replacing the cards in their box.

'About what?'

'That last hand. You didn't have to make such a fool of her.'

'I squoze her. What's wrong with that?'

'You watched her face before you bid; you knew she had openers; you made an outrageous bid you knew she'd double; you even re-doubled; then you bluffed her by discarding your queen on her ace; and you enjoyed making her look idiotic.'

'All's fair in love and war.'

'Not when you're at war and she's in love.'

Robbie was unrepentant. 'I like winning; I like squeezing; and with whom, may I ask, is our Margaret in love?'

'You *know* who she's in love with. And stop changing the subject. You didn't have to call a slam. Five diamonds would have given you game and rubber.'

'I wouldn't have made five diamonds. I had a string

of diamonds and a void in clubs. Margaret had an opening bid, which had to be in spades and clubs. If it was
spades, you probably had a void—'

'I had a singleton.'

'So, if I'm in five, she risks leading her king of spades
after the ace; you discard; she leads another; you trump
– and I'm down. The only contract I had a chance of
making was a little slam. And it was the only contract
worth making.'

'Because it was a gamble?'

'A challenged! It's all I've got left, the freedom to challenge: don't begrudge me it.'

'That why you're provoking Cheadle all along the
line?'

Robbie grinned. 'Against Cheadle I'm playing three
handed bridge, with you the third. I've called a grand
slam, I'm vulnerable and he's got two aces; but I'm
going to make him discard them both. That first lead of
yours – dumping Miss Talbot at the Rex – has given me
my contract.'

'And what,' demanded Mark, 'are his two aces?'

'He knows who the murderer is,' whispered Robbie,
mockingly dramatic, 'and who's protecting him.' He
glanced at the clock. 'Bloody hell, look at the time. Tell
you what: while I'm cleaning my teeth, you pour us a
nightcap and we'll drink to the success of tomorrow's
grand slam.'

'Go clean your teeth,' Mark ordered, nodding; but,
as he watched Robbie wheel himself into the bathroom,
knew that he dare not risk tomorrow's game. Whatever
Robbie thought, the chief superintendent had intuition as
well as logic. And whatever Robbie might squeeze him
into discarding, it would not be *both* his aces. So the game
must be cancelled.

Pouring two large tots of whisky, he emptied the contents of six phenobarb capsules into the glass he held for Robbie – which rhythmically he swirled. Later, he would get the rubber tube he kept in his car for siphoning, and the funnel, put the tube down Robbie's throat, and pour into his gut a solution of warm water and all the remaining phenobarbs.

He heard his brother flush the toilet and, turning to face the bathroom, stood with a glass in either hand.

Robbie rolled up to him and accepted the glass he proffered.

Mark raised his glass. 'Sleep well,' he murmured.

'To my grand slam,' Robbie toasted, peering mischievously at Mark through the whisky. Then hesitated, scowling; and held his glass to the light, at arm's length. 'Strange,' he announced, 'this whisky's full of sediment.' He set down his glass on the low table. 'You must ask for your money back.' And wheeled himself swiftly to his bedroom, whose door he promptly shut.

Recovering his wits, Mark ran up the hall and turned the knob of the door; but once again it was locked.

'Robbie,' he shouted, knocking.

'What?'

'We've *got* to talk.'

'Tomorrow,' Robbie called back. 'When I'll do all the talking.'

FRIDAY: EIGHT A.M.

Cheadle washed the remnants of his shaving cream off his face; dried his face and hands; dabbed some brilliantine on the palm of his hand; rubbed both palms together and slicked them backwards over his grey hair. Which then, meticulously, he combed.

Replacing his comb in his jacket pocket, he examined his face in the mirror. He looked fresh – in spite of the fact that he had had no sleep the night before – and he felt pleased with himself. Because today, unless he was sadly mistaken, he was going to wrap up the case of the Motorway Maniac. And, what was more, wrap it up as no police officer had wrapped up a murder enquiry before.

There were a few more facts he needed, of course; but he had no doubt they'd arrive before the day was out. Actually, timing was going to matter more than facts. He must enter that cottage at precisely the right moment; and from that moment on must time perfectly every word and move. One slip and the Gifford boys'd have him up a gum tree.

They were a fascinating pair, he reflected as he walked to his headquarters. The sailor laddie so honest he'd only been able to tell two lies; but so resourceful he could brazen his way into a local cinema with a corpse in a wheelchair. And the paraplegic laddie so brilliant under interrogation that almost every word had had two meanings. Except his insults, which had been singularly explicit. It had been a positive treat to read Sergeant Robinson's transcribed record of all he'd said. A real display of wordmanship.

Cheadle grinned as he remembered Robbie's violent shifts from frivolity to rudeness, abandon to acquiescence, obstructiveness to co-operation. All apparently spontaneous : yet each cunningly contrived to irk and bedazzle.

Yet it would be Master Robert who'd make the mistake. No one could go on giving every word two meanings, and switching moods, and playing the police at their own game, without, in the end, making a mistake. Oscar Wilde had proved that.

Master Mark, on the other hand, would stick doggedly to the truth – except on the subject of kips and short trips up the lane to see if his engine was running more smoothly. Would not only stick to the truth but would feel no embarrassment at answering slowly and unimaginatively. Master Mark would make the police prove everything.

Master Robert, on the other hand, would admit everything – and laugh when no one could prove a word of it.

Soon, however, the doggedness of the one stimulating the recklessness of the other, Robbie would go too far. At which precise moment he, Cheadle, must begin the final dialogue.

'Sergeant,' he called. Sergeant Robinson appeared instantly. 'I know it's almost killing you, sitting dumb while I ask all the questions, but you've got to keep it up. It alarms Master Mark and infuriates Master Robert. Which is just how I want them.' He glanced at his notebook. 'Oh yes. Before we visit the Gifford boys, remind me to see Miss Margaret. I'm interested in last night's game of bridge.'

FRIDAY: HALF PAST TWO

For the sixth or seventh time on what had been a grey, drizzly day, Mark knocked at his brother's door; and for the sixth or seventh time, there was no answer. At two hourly intervals throughout the night he had heard the shrilling of Robbie's alarm; this morning, from the front lawn, peering through the bedroom window, he had seen him sitting moodily in his chair; at midday he had offered, unavailingly, to cook him a meal; and now he knocked again.

'Robbie,' he shouted, 'for God's sake, you've been there almost twenty-four hours. At least let me give you something to drink.'

'You gave me something to drink last night!' reminded Robbie, breaking his silence at last.

'Robbie, please come out.'

'Not till Cheadle arrives.'

'That'll be too late and you know it. We've got to talk before he arrives; we can't do it through a locked door.'

Again there was silence; but of a different quality. Thoughtful rather than surly.

'I'll come out,' Robbie finally agreed, 'if you go down to the end of the garden—'

'What the hell for?'

'So you can't jump me. Go right down the garden and shout when you get there. And keep shouting.'

'I can't just stand at the bottom of the garden shouting.'

'Sing then. Do what you like, so long as I can hear you and be sure you're not lurking.'

'And if I do, you'll come out and talk?'

'I'll talk from the garden door. Rush me, though, and I'll slide it to and lock it.'

'I've no intention of rushing you.'

'Glad to hear it.'

'I'm off now.' Robbie heard him walking down the hall. 'Mark!'

'What?'

'Take the target with you. I might as well kill *two* birds!'

'I'll shout when I've set it up.'

'Do that.'

Robbie – a sports jacket over his light summer shirt, a rug over his legs – wheeled himself to the locked door. And heard his brother's distant shout. But did not move. Refrained even from unlocking his door. Just listened – and heard nothing. Until, raucously self-conscious, Mark's voice sang that all the birds in the air were a'sighing and a'sobbing.

Silently laughing, Robbie unlocked his door and pushed himself down the hall.

'*Who*, Mark was demanding of a deserted and derisive countryside, '*killed Cock Robin?*'

Robbie put his bow across the arms of his chair, his quivered arrows over his shoulder.

> '*I, said the sparrow,*
> *with my bow and arrow,*
> *I killed Cock Robin.*
> *And all the birds of the air*
> *fell a'sighing and a'sobbing. . . .*'

'All right,' Robbie called from the doorway, sidling

his chair, locking the wheels, 'you can stop now.'

When they heard of the death . . '

'That's enough!'

. . . *'Of poor Cock Robin.'*

An arrow hissed over Mark's shoulder and thudded into the target. 'I said,' rasped Robbie, 'that's enough. Now move aside. And whatever it is you want to say, say it from there, while I practise.'

'I wanted to say I'm sorry about last night; and about Wednesday night; and to tell you even if you *had* started to drink that whisky, I'd have stopped you.'

A second arrow thudded into the target – a gold.

'Probably you don't believe me,' Mark continued. . . .

'I do.'

'Doesn't matter anyway. What matters is Cheadle. Robbie, don't try it. Leave all the running to him. Just do what you said – make sure he hasn't enough to arrest me.'

A third arrow hissed and thudded. A second gold.

'And if I do?'

'I promise you, you'll be safe.'

'Safe maybe' – drawing his bow a fourth time – 'but plagued by coppers.' His bow at full stretch, quite steady. 'They'll never let up. You know that.' And at last released the arrow. Not a gold. 'Blast!'

'But it's the best we can hope for. Isn't it?'

Robbie grinned, drew and shot – almost without aiming – and scored a third gold.

'That's better,' he commented. 'Come inside.'

'You've only shot five.'

'The sixth I'll keep handy. Now, nice and slow – no, slower than that – come inside. We'll finish our talk in here.' And, as a Mark slowly paced towards him, withdrew, locking his chair so that it was side on both to the garden door and to the arm-chair on the left of the fireplace.

Deliberately then, as Mark came through the door, he raised his bow and drew back the sixth arrow. 'Sit,' he ordered, nodding at the arm-chair in front of which he berthed. 'Sit very carefully.'

Instead, Mark halted, surprised that he felt no fear. Because he knew that Robbie intended to kill him. Knew also that he must either sit and be killed, or at once attempt to escape.

'Sit,' Robbie urged him, his voice gently firm.

He could run, or fling himself sideways, or dive for cover behind the arm-chair. Any of them would give Robbie a difficult shot.

'You'll not move an inch in any direction before this arrow's through your heart,' Robbie promised, the arched bow wickedly steady. 'My neck's fine, my arm's strong and my eye's never been better. Now *sit.*' And even – so confident was he – risked dipping his bow until the arrow pointed into the arm-chair beside him.

Mark's lack of fear gave way to a strangely passive curiosity. About what? he wondered, stepping towards the arm-chair. Certainly not about death.

'Steady,' Robbie instructed. 'Go very steady, kiddo. Now turn around.' Mark about-turned, his broad back to the arrow's sharp head. Not about death: about Robbie. 'Reach back with your hand.' He reached back, and felt the arm-chair. About whether Robbie could really do it. He sidled round the chair, halted and, turning to face Robbie, found the point not of an arrow but of a sabre touching his chest.

'I switched,' Robbie teased, 'while your back was turned. You could've got clean away.' He prodded a little, the sabre pricking bare tanned skin where the shirt lay open. 'Sit.'

Mark sat, the sabre an inch from his chest; and running

down his chest a glistening of blood. But still he felt only passivity and curiosity.

'Cushions!' Robbie accused. 'And phenobarbs! "I'll turn you tonight",' he mimicked angrily. 'You'd have turned me all right. Straight into me grave.'

'What are you planning?' Mark asked.

'You know.'

Mark shook his head. 'Don't be stupid, Robbie.'

'Whatever else I may be,' Robbie assured him, dangerously provoked, 'I'm never stupid.'

'Not so far, no. In fact quite clever. At times.'

'And what do we mean by that?'

'I was thinking of Margaret and Annabel, and even Diana. Crafty the way you laid 'em and got rid of 'em so's only I suspected.'

'Of course.'

'Sad thing is, they were only something to take out when you went out. I only came home to see you. So you needn't have bothered laying any of them. Or did you, at the age of nineteen and twenty and twenty-one respectively, enjoy seducing them away from your little brother?'

'No more,' shrugged Robbie, 'then I enjoyed seducing away the angelic Dibbs Minor when I was only sweet eighteen.'

'In his case, though, seducing wasn't enough, was it? You had to get *him* expelled as well.'

'I merely advised your housemaster that he wasn't coming up to London to see his dentist, as he claimed : he was coming, uninvited and unwanted, to pester me at my digs. And I only did it because I knew you were his friend and I didn't want you getting into trouble. Dibbs Minor, little brother, was a whore.'

'He asked for permission to go to his dentist,' Mark refuted wearily, 'because you put him up to it. He was besotted with you.'

Taken aback, Robbie asked: 'And just when did you realize that? That I put him up to it, I mean.'

'Wednesday.'

Robbie nodded. 'Ah yes. And I can tell you the exact moment. It was after I'd shot so badly. You were putting the target back against the wall; I asked you, "how's the toothache?" and for a moment you couldn't even remember you'd told me you'd slept too late to go to your dentist. You hesitated. So subconsciously you'd picked for me the lie I'd picked for Dibbs Minor. And when I asked you how your toothache was, you subconsciously remembered where first you'd heard it. And last night, after bridge, you even had the indelicacy to bring it out in the open.'

'I didn't mean to be indelicate: I was trying to get through to you.'

'Too late now.'

'You say you're never stupid,' Mark mused; 'but what could be stupider than getting yourself arrested for murdering me?'

'I'm not going to murder you,' Robbie protested. 'I'm accidentally going to kill you.'

Scorn displaced curiosity. 'People sitting in chairs don't get accidentally killed with sabres, Robbie. With shotguns maybe; but with sabres?

'Which is why, when you're dead,' Robbie countered, 'I'll lift your legs, pull you across the arms of my chair, shove this sixth arrow into your chest where the sabre went in, and dump you down by the target. You see, little brother, people in the vicinity of targets *do* get accidentally killed by arrows.'

'You think the police'll think that?'

'No. They'll think the Motorway Maniac committed suicide. From remorse. Or because he knew his arrest was imminent.'

'And what'll you tell them? How'll you, a master bowman, explain away shooting someone yards to the right of your target?'

'Yards to the right? I'll do no such thing : my pride'd never let me. No, you're going to be shot, according to the Gospel of St Robert, bang in front of the gold. There's three in the gold already : you'll have precluded my fourth.'

'What'll you *tell* them?' Mark persisted.

'I'll tell them you set up the target, stood to one side, watched me shoot five, and then – just as I loosed off my sixth – to my horror – stepped straight into the line of flight. "Why'd he *do* it?" I'll groan. "Do you think he thought I'd fired half a dozen?" And then Cheadle'll explain. He'll stand in front of the fire-place there, his shoes as shiny as the arse of his pants, his hair slicked down like President Johnson's, and he'll say, "Now, now, Mr Robert, you mustn't blame yourself. You did all you could to protect him; but he *was* a murderer, you know, and he did know the net was closing.'

Mark nodded, no longer curious, simply wanting it done with. But Robbie was not to be hurried.

'What else can I do?' he demanded. 'You'll kill me if I don't kill you. And I can't protect myself day and night, can I? And what's the alternative? Let Cheadle arrest you? See you in the dock as the Motorway Maniac? Wait for Margaret to come and tell me you've been put away for life—?'

'You said the police'd *never* arrest me.' Robbie had protested too much and Mark's passivity had yielded at last to an aggrieved desire to live. 'You said they'd never get a conviction because they'd never find a motive.'

'Well I'm afraid I misjudged them. They've established you were on the scene of each crime at each of the relevant times, and that you had access, here, to all the props you needed for your stunt at the Rex. That's opportunity and method; and obviously they're going to rely on them alone. Purely circumstantial; but they don't seem to care. It'll be a case of Evans and Hanratty all over again.'

'You're forgetting my alibi.'

'My phone calls? They'll soon break that.'

'You'll tell them I didn't answer?'

'Of course not. But Charlie will; and so'll the Liptons. Because I told both, at the time, that I hadn't got you.'

'But you have got me, haven't you?

'Cheadle has.'

'Robbie, don't underestimate Cheadle. I know you'll think I'm only saying that because I'm frightened—'

'And you aren't?'

'Terrified, actually. Specially' – nodding at the sabre – 'of that.'

'You'll feel nothing.'

'Make no odds if I do : I'll be dead. But you . . . they'll get you.'

'Never. They're not due here for at least two hours; I've got plenty of time; and I've worked it all out.'

'They'll still get you. Then it'll be you, in that chair, in prison, for the rest of your life, with nothing to make it bearable. There'll be no archery for you in prison, Robbie. No javelin throwing, or fencing, or medals, or cars, or privacy—'

'Stop it!' Robbie shouted, so shaken that even the blade of his sabre trembled. He took a deep, shuddering breath : then continued quietly but implacably : 'It's no use, kiddo : we've gone too far – you, me, and Cheadle.'

'There's is an alternative.'

'What?'

'Let me stay and look after you.'

'You'd look after me all right!'

'Don't.'

'Sorry. A bit cheap.' And for the first time looked ill

at ease, disconcerted by his own bad manners, the coldness
of his expression thawing visibly under a flush of irritation.

Observing his brother's embarrassment, Mark realized
that he had almost won a reprieve. A few more persuasive
words. . . . 'We'd be happy,' he promised. 'Plenty of
bridge; someone to help you with the boring chores,
turn you at night occasionally, go to the flicks with.
Things'd be easier for you. You'd win every medal going
at the Olympics. . . .

A mistake! For Robbie there'd be no Olympics; and
both of them knew it.

'We've gone too far,' Robbie repeated, his face stony.
'We're going on.

'Then get it over and done with.

'Soon,' Robbie promised. 'But in my time, not yours.
Yesterday you told me I should respect the police, remember?

'But Cheadle arrived so you couldn't tell me why you
didn't. Yes, I remember. Go on.' Impatient to die.

'Well it all began,' Robbie related, comfortably, 'late
one night when I was four. I was asleep, as all good
children of four should be late at night, when suddenly
something – I didn't know what – woke me. I sat up, terrified, and there, on the big double bed across the other
side of that grotty little room, were my dear papa and
my sainted mama' – gulping – 'naked and writhing and
tearing at one another, him forcing her down, holding
her spreadeagled with his hands and his knees, and her
screaming, her head threshing from side to side.'

Now all the colour had gone from his face and his
eyes, inward looking, were blind. Shove the blade aside,
Mark thought; but was transfixed by his brother's unsee-
ing eyes. Which suddenly focused, aborting hope.

'That's what woke me,' Robbie explained. 'My mother
screaming "no" and "stop" and "bastard" and "you're

too, big, you're hurting me" her head threshing and him pinning her down, spreadeagled, while he humped her – only I didn't realize that that's all it was.'

It would have been easy then to disarm him. Instead, the blade forgotten, Mark muttered : 'Oh, Robbie.'

Robbie nodded. 'I thought he was killing her. I shouted leave her alone; but he didn't. Didn't even hear me, come to that. And neither did she. So then' – again that shuddering inhalation – 'I tried to pull him off her. . . . He stopped his humping just long enough to snarl piss off and went straight back to killing her.'

With the thumb and little finger of his free hand he pressed at his temples, as if to obliterate the memory inside his skull. 'I was petrified. Not for myself. For her. He looked so huge, and pitiless, and I couldn't think what to . . . so I jumped on his back. He didn't miss a beat. Just bucked me off.

'I grabbed his hair then : started yanking. And still not missing a beat, he back-handed me on to the floor, all the time my mother writhing and moaning and begging him "No, Angus, no, *please*, you're hurting," So back, battered but undaunted I went. And sank my sharp little teeth into the first thing I saw. Which happened to be his arse.

'He missed a beat then all right! Reared up, grabbed my neck with one hand, a leg with the other, lifted me over his head, and threw me.' Robbie was smiling now : telling a story against himself. 'I flew across the room, bounced off the edge of the table, landed on the floor and was just about to start screaming the place down when my mother shouted "And bloody stay there."

'Which I did, for the simple reason I couldn't move. And I didn't scream because I couldn't feel. I just lay there. While they got at it again.'

He pressed his diaphragm and coughed. 'Seemed hours

till they stopped and my mother came to look at me. They had a cigarette first, I remember. And when she did come to me all she could say, 'cos I'd started crying, was 'Stop that bloody snivelling.'

'More to the point, though, my father told me to get back to my bed. I couldn't, of course; which got me another hammering. In the end, though, they dropped to it that something was wrong : so my father got dressed and went out to phone for an ambulance. And while he was out, my mother told me : 'You fell down the stairs, do you hear? You were sneaking out, while your father and me was asleep, and you fell down the stairs. You tell the doctor anything else and I promise you, Robbie, I'll murder you.'

'So I told the doctor I'd fallen down the stairs. And I told the N.S.P.C.C. I'd fallen down the stairs. And the N.S.P.C.C. told the police it was the most blatant bit of child battering they'd seen in years, only they couldn't prove it unless the police got either my father or my mother to talk.

'And here, little brother, we come to the moral of this pretty tale. Do you know what the police did?' Mark shook his head. 'They did nothing. And *you* tell *me* to re*spect* them' – jabbing three times with his sabre, drawing a seed pearl of blood each time.

Which Mark ignored, asking simply : 'Why've you never told me before?'

Robbie looked surprised. 'Never told anyone. At first because I wasn't prepared to admit that my father and mother couldn't stand me : then because I thought I wanted to forget; and finally, when that bump on the squash court finished what my father had begun, because I found that what I really wanted was to keep it all to myself – and feed on it. So I did. And feeding on it's given me the strength to endure this ridiculous life.'

'What about your devoted voice from Houston?'

'I told you, kiddo : you gave my life direction. But my fuel' – his sabre arm tensing – 'was hate. And now, I'm afraid' – inching the sabre backwards, lining it up – 'it's time for splashdown.'

'Not yet,' Mark murmured, glancing over Robbie's shoulder, warning him. 'We've got company.'

And Robbie, turning slowly round, saw Cheadle in the hall doorway.

'Hello, Superintendent,' he greeted heartily, laying aside his sabre. 'You turn up at the most *in*convenient times, don't you?'

Cheadle grinned. And not merely with relief : he was genuinely amused. He had been standing out of sight in the hall for the past three minutes, and it had not really required that '*Now*' urgently whispered through the miniature receiver he had clamped to his ear to impel him round the corner into the room. The way Master Robert had said 'splashdown' had done that. Yet instantly the same Master Robert had made him laugh.

Quite a boy. No more of a boy, though, than his brother. Because Master Mark, showing lots of white teeth in an easy smile, had just risen to greet him as if he were a captain barging uninvited into the second officer's cabin.

Wryly shaking his head, Cheadle gave the Gifford brothers his well practised saddened look; and was unsurprised to observe that it had no effect at all. Master Mark, casually rubbing his bare chest, continued to smile politely : Master Robert attacked with bravura rudeness.

'Still getting nowhere fast?' Robbie taunted.

'I had to get *here* rather fast,' Cheadle riposted. 'Do you know what one of my men radio-ed through to me on his walkie-talkie? That you were about to kill your brother.'

'Now what,' wondered Robbie, 'could possibly have

made him think that? And where is this walking-talking
man of yours? Up my chimney?'

'Up that tree,' Cheadle corrected, pointing to an elm
beyond the hedge. 'With a pair of field glasses. We
thought it wise. You seemed to know so much, and be so
vulnerable. Was my man mistaken?'

Robbie turned ironically to Mark. 'Was his man mistaken?'

'Am I dead?' asked Mark, matching his brother's
irony, his smile now maddeningly amused.

'It seems,' Robbie pronounced, 'your man was mistaken.'
The sergeant tapped on the glass door. 'Come in, Charlie.
I was just telling Cheadle here that his man was mistaken.
It wasn't you, was it? No, of course it wasn't : you can't
talk ! Anyway, you've come on a fool's errand. Which is
nothing if not apt.'

It was going to be a dirty battle, Cheadle realized,
almost wishing he could offer quarter, but incapable of
doing so. He was a hunter. Licensed, but a hunter. Of
men. Also, Robbie had just called him Cheadle. Not even
Mister Cheadle, like some of the cockier villains. Just
plain, unadorned Cheadle. 'Come in Charlie,' he'd said,
'I was just telling *Cheadle* here his man was mistaken.'

Right, Master Robert, thought Cheadle, we'll soon see
who's mistaken. And, smiling submissively, said : 'We
meant well, sir. And my man couldn't see your face as
clearly as all that.'

'Pity,' Robbie assured him, turning his head to the
right. 'This profile's perfect.'

'But he thought your *brother* looked terrified. Got a
very good view of him moving backwards into that chair.
And was sure he was terrified.'

'My brother's an extremely brave man,' snapped Robbie, to both Cheadle's and Mark's surprise. 'He'd never
have looked terrified.'

Cheadle looked at Mark. 'Why were you backing round the chair, sir?' he asked.

'A childish habit I can't get out of,' Mark assured him, playing it Robbie's way, touched by Robbie's loyalty.

'And why were you jabbing Mr Mark with a sword?' Cheadle asked Robbie.

'I was practising my thrusts,' said Robbie virtuously. 'And it's a sabre not a sword.'

'And what were you saying as you practised your thrusts?'

'Can't your walking-talking, tree-climbing man read lips?'

'I'm afraid not.'

'As you should be, because now you'll never know the fascinating story of my extraordinary life.'

'Does one brother tell another the story of his extraordinary life?'

'If there are parts of it the other doesn't know.'

'In your case, I suppose,' Cheadle ventured, firing a first ranging shot, 'that would be the fascinating part before you were adopted?'

'And how,' Robbie demanded coldly, refusing to take cover, 'did you find out about that?'

'Miss Margaret let it slip – that you were only an "adopted" Gifford, I mean – when I saw her at lunch-time. I called on her just to say goodbye – the case'll be closed by this evening and I'll be returning to London tomorrow – and we talked a little. She's a nice lass. She thinks you think she's a half wit.'

'Can't imagine why.'

'Oh, things like that little slam you called last night.'

Robbie looked both surprised and uncertain. 'You play bridge?'

Cheadle nodded. 'Rather well, as a matter of fact. You wouldn't have got that slam if the lead had been mine.'

All Robbie's uncertainty vanished. 'If the lead had been yours, I wouldn't have called it, you twit. Against you, I'd have waited. Till I could call seven.' Conspiratorially, he winked at Mark.

'Pity we won't have time for a game,' regretted Cheadle, who knew nothing about bridge except the jargon he'd picked up from Margaret.

'But aren't we playing now?' asked Robbie slyly.

'In a manner of speaking, sir, I suppose we are.'

'Let's make the contract seven then. In spades,' Robbie challenged.

'Spades?' queried Cheadle.

'Doesn't the queen of spades mean death?'

'Ah,' said Cheadle, understanding at last, accepting the challenge, 'of course.'

'You realize, don't you, that Mark's your partner, the first lead was his and half the hand's been played?'

'I realize that, sir.'

'Did you double? I can't remember.'

'No, sir.' – recalling all that Margaret had told him, and glibly regurgitating. 'You're vulnerable and it's a friendly game : I don't care for penalty points.'

'How very chivalrous. All right : you were saying that I was adopted.'

'Yes. So I had one of my men follow it up—'

'You must have a lot of men.'

'Fifty actually. Not to mention the co-operation of every other Force in the kingdom.'

'Good for you. And what did your man come up with?'

'The N.S.P.C.C.'s report on the case of a four-year-old Glaswegian called Robert Stephen Thomson – yourself.'

'Your interest in my childhood trauma touches me not at all : it comes a quarter of a century too late. But what else, pray, have your fifty men and the co-operating Forces of the entire kingdom come up with?'

'The P & O Company advised one of them that **Mr Mark** was a most resourceful officer. Another got the facts about your television set. And still others checked with Stoke Mandeville's Chief Physiotherapist and Mr and Mrs Stanley Lipton on the subject of those telephone calls which were your brother's alibi for several rather vital hours on Wednesday.'

'Oh dear.'

'Yes, you haven't exactly been truthful with us, have you?'

'In my position, what would you have done?'

'Lied probably; but may we now have the truth?'

'Try me.'

Instead, and with blatant insincerity, Cheadle asked: 'Warm enough, are you sir?'

'I told you, we don't *feel* the cold. And even if we did, with this on' – tugging at the lapel of his jacket – 'I wouldn't.' But for all his tartness, Robbie was disconcerted by Cheadle's change of pace.

'Glad to hear it,' Cheadle assured him with even less sincerity. Then rapped: 'Now, when you made those phone calls here on Wednesday, to whom, in fact, did you speak?'

'To no one.' Robbie looked sullen.

'And why was that, would you say?'

'Mark sleeps like a log. Sailors do, you know: through typhoon and tempest till duty calls. Probably he didn't hear the phone.'

Cheadle cocked his head at Mark. 'Do you sleep like a log, sir?'

'I do. And I didn't hear the phone.'

Cheadle grinned again. Mr Mark as ever, was sticking to the literal truth. He doubtless did sleep soundly; and

'Otherwise I can't condone my brother being sent to Broadmoor.'

'You mean, you'd *sell* your brother's freedom?'

'I mean, I'm not being paid to destroy it.'

'But you were about to destroy it this afternoon! My walking-talking-tree-climbing man saw you at it.'

'To save him from Broadmoor. I knew you were coming to make an arrest; and I knew you didn't care any longer that you can't prove motive.'

'To be frank, I don't,' Cheadle confessed indifferently : but his heart was singing. Master Robert had said too much – without even realizing it. Soon he'd make a mistake. 'And you're right : I couldn't even begin to prove your brother's motive.'

'Exactly. So I had to save him from arrest.'

'And would you have confessed the method whereby you'd saved him?'

'I would not. You'd have found him in front of my target, an arrow through his heart and me in hysterics because I'd accidentally killed him.'

'Accidentally?'

'Look at the target.' Obediently Cheadle looked. 'How many arrows in it?'

'Er . . . five.'

'Bowmen shoot six. I'd have told you Mark must've miscounted and stepped into the line of fire just as I shot my last. And you, of course, would have decided it was suicide.'

'I wonder.'

'Well, at the time you may have wondered; but as time passed, and there were no more motorway murders, you'd have decided it must have been suicide after all.'

'Ah yes, of course. Of course I would. How very clever of you, sir,' he congratulated gratefully. Grateful for the long awaited mistake. He turned amiably to Mark. 'Just as well I arrived when I did, then, isn't it? I'd never have been forgiven if I'd let you be killed. Capital punishment that would have been. And that's a relic of our barbarous past, isn't it?'

'Obviously one whose passing you regret,' Mark smouldered.

'No, not entirely. The passing of hangmen, as practitioners of judicial homicide, I don't regret; but your brother's solution – suicide –' Cheadle gestured to indicate that, in his opinion, in certain cases, there was a lot to be said for a guilty man's judicial suicide. Gestured; but left the thought unspoken.

Understanding perfectly, Mark scowled. 'Where do we go from here?' he asked. 'To the station? With a blanket over my head?'

'Now talking of heads,' responded Cheadle, unhurriedly, 'when you entered the Rex, were you wearing the wig we subsequently found on the dead girl's head?'

'I was.'

'And did you choose the Rex because, as Mr Robert pointed out, that put the Maniac's mark on Miss Talbot's death?'

'I did.'

'And when I asked had you seen anyone on the A.41 pick up any girl, and you said no, did you lie?'

For fully fifteen seconds Mark considered how best to reply: then said slowly: 'I didn't see *myself* pick up a girl.'

'But you did pick one up?'

'Yes.'

'At what time?'

'I suppose about five to three.'

'Was she alone?'

'Yes.'

'Are you married?'

'No.'

'Engaged?'

'No.'

'Girl friend?'

'Mind your own business.'

'He never,' explains Robbie, 'talks sex.'

But Cheadle's eyes remained on Mark's. 'When exactly did you work out the details of your plan to deposit Miss Talbot in the Rex?'

'After Robbie had left for Stoke.'

'Only then?'

'I could hardly do it while he was here.'

'Did you, at any time before you wheeled her into the Rex, remove her from your car?'

'I brought her in here.'

'Why?'

'It was too dangerous to leave her in my car. Someone might have called. Anyway, I had to work out a plan.'

'In the process of which, you spilt her perfume?'

'Yes.'

'Did you bring the others here?'

Again Mark hesitated, almost as if he had not understood the question; but finally enquired : 'You don't really expect me to tell you about them, do you?'

'Not really, no. Except you did tell us about Miss Talbot.'

'You knew about her.'

'Have done,' Cheadle confirmed, 'ever since you and Mr Robert turned up outside the Rex and my sergeant smelt that perfume. On you! In fourteen months, that was our first break. And I was so grateful to you I followed it up myself.'

At last he turned to Robbie. 'Yours has been a difficult rôle, hasn't it, sir?'

Robbie bridled. 'Don't patronize me, Cheadle.'

'Now how could I, Mr Gifford? We both started life in the gutter. Me in the East End, you in the Gorbals. And even though we've both succeeded since, your accent disguises your origins far better than mine does mine. I mean, you'd never say toilet, sir, would you? You'd say lavatory.'

'Water closet, actually,' drawled Robbie.

'But, of course, water closet. Whereas I'd say W.C. So how could I possibly patronise you? No, I genuinely mean it: yours has been a very tricky rôle. And you've played it superbly, sir.'

'I don't know what you're talking about,' Robbie disclaimed.

'Well, your various hints to us about your brother's guilt, for one thing. You had to tell us just enough to frighten him, but not enough to let us arrest him, didn't you?'

'I thought if I could stop him killing, and at the same time keep him out of your hands, I was justified,' amended Robbie.

'But in case we didn't get the message, you told the Chief Physiotherapist and the Liptons that your brother had just arrived here, but you couldn't raise him by telephone?'

'Yes.'

'So that, if the worst came to the worst, and you had to prove to us that your brother *could* have left Miss Talbot at the Rex, you could refer us to the Chief Physiotherapist and the Liptons?'

'Yes.'

'But at that time, on Wednesday afternoon, when you spoke to the Chief Physiotherapist and the Liptons, *you didn't even know* that your brother had a dead girl in his car! I asked you. And you said no, all you'd seen was five Pakistanis in the boot.'

Robbie threw up his hands. 'Of course I did. He's my brother for Christ's sake. For the twentieth time, he's my brother.'

'You mean, you lied for him about that, too?'

'I mean,' Robbie sulked, 'I saw her body on the front seat of his car as I wheeled past it to get into my own.'

'Sitting bolt upright, was she?'

'At first I only saw her hat. A big purple thing sticking up against the window. And I thought, that's odd: Mark doesn't wear big purple hats! So I opened the door. And there she was, lying along the front seat, on her back, bleeding slightly from a wound in the midriff, but very dead.'

'Well, yes, she would have been. The murder weapon entered the body just below the breast bone, travelled unimpeded upwards and killed her instantly. Same as the three other girls.' He looked at his notes – not reading – waiting – breaking the rhythm of their dialogue. 'Why do you think your brother murdered these four girls?'

'I doubt he knows himself.'

'But you were determined he shouldn't stand trial?'

'Yes.'

Giving the impression that he found nothing unreasonable about that, Cheadle reverted to Mark. 'Do you believe what your brother says, sir?'

'He'd never have let me stand trial,' Mark agreed.

'Do you know why?'

'Yes.'

'Mr Robert' – Cheadle asked rather more deliberately – 'were you afraid of your brother simply because *he* knew *you* knew that Janine Talbot's body was in his car when you left here for Stoke on Wednesday afternoon?'

'I became afraid,' Robbie answered, with equal deliberation, 'only when he convinced me he was planning to kill me.'

'But Miss Margaret tells me he's devoted to you.'

'He was still planning to kill me. On Wednesday night I saw him rehearsing it, with a pillow; and last night he offered me a nightcap full of phenobarbs.'

'So *he's* tried to kill you; and *you,* when I came in this afternoon, were about to kill him?'

'We were always,' Robbie smiled, 'a close family.'

But Cheadle did not smile back. He felt like a juggler with ten balls in the air who knew that to relax for an instant would be to drop the lot and disgrace himself. Anyway, it was time to catch Mr Mark again.

'*Did* you try to kill your brother?' he asked Mark.

'I thought about it.'

'Twice, if I'm to believe Mr Robert?'

'I thought about it twice.'

'Why?'

'You're asking me for my motive?'

'Yes.'

'Isn't motive your job?'

'All right,' sighed Cheadle, adding a further ball to the ten he was already keeping in fluent flight : 'try this for size. You committed this series of murders close to your brother's home in the confident expectation that suspicion would eventually fall on him?'

Mark stayed silent, waiting for the whole of the question; but Robbie exploded.

'Not even you,' he shouted at Cheadle, 'are stupid enough to believe a cripple capable of bumping off four able-bodied girls and disposing of their four able bodies here, there and everywhere.'

As if he had never spoken, Cheadle resumed his theorising, still aiming it at Mark, itemising each point. 'You stabbed each girl as she sat beside you in your car – knowing that even a cripple could do that.

'Later, at times when it could easily be established that

Mr Robert was alone, because you were en route to your cousins, you bundled each of the first three girls out of your car, as it was moving, under cover of darkness, in the vicinity of a police station – knowing that a cripple as strong and determined as your brother could also do that.

'And finally, when we'd failed to identify your brother as the maniac after three killings, you committed a fourth, disposed of the body in a manner befitting the maniac but then, very clumsily, drew our attention to yourself. So clumsily you hoped to convince us that you were merely an accessory. A devoted accessory ridding his murderous brother of an unwanted corpse, in fact. And that at a time when aforesaid murderous brother, being elsewhere, seemed to have an alibi.

'But it was all too pat, Mr Mark. I mean, why did you return to the Rex stinking of the dead girl's perfume? Why, if it wasn't to lead us back here to your brother?

'You having led us back, your brother, of course, began to protect himself. By dropping hints to all and sundry. But that didn't worry you : because the more he hinted, the more he appeared to be attempting merely to incriminate you, his accessory.

'Which left you free to kill him, either with a pillow or with phenobarbs, and then to tell us, "I had to do it : I couldn't let you imprison a brother both dear to me and crippled." Now what do you say to that?'

His discourse concluded, all eleven balls once more safely in hand, Cheadle sat back complacently, demanding applause.

'Clever!' Robbie applauded sarcastically. 'Clever Mark, clever copper! You deserve each other.'

But Mark, still stolidly appraising the question, said nothing. It would be necessary, Cheadle decided, to rattle him.

'How much did your father leave you, sir?' he asked, his tone contemptuous.

Mark frowned. 'Leave me? About twenty thousand.'

'Actually,' Cheadle corrected, 'twenty-one thousand pounds and fifty-eight pence. Net. We've checked. And he left it to you on the understanding that you'd provide for your brother?'

'Of course.'

'How much has your brother – ' gesturing comprehensively at the room in which they sat, and at everything beyond it – 'cost you so far?'

'About eight and a half thousand.'

'And how much a year do you allow Mr Robert?'

'Fifteen hundred. After tax.'

'After tax, eh? So that, even if your remaining ten thousand is well invested, in seven years time at the most there'll be nothing left?'

'So what?'

'So if you murdered him this leave, and got away with it, you'd be ten thousand better off than if you let him live. How's that for a motive?'

'Absurd,' Mark told him promptly.

'Why?'

'Because he's only got –'

And, furious with himself for his carelessness, with Cheadle for his deviousness, swallowed the rest of the sentence.

'Exactly,' said Cheadle.

Mark thought hard and clearly. Then challenged: 'I don't believe you've got a warrant at all.'

'Sorry, sir,' said Cheadle; and even contrived to look sorry as he withdrew a document from an inside pocket.

'Show me,' Mark demanded.

Watched intently by Robbie, Cheadle handed across

the document : which Mark perused. 'I want to confess,' he announced.

'But Mr Gifford,' Cheadle began.

Mark swept him aside. 'Take it down, Sergeant' – returning the warrant, which Cheadle, reluctantly, slid back into his pocket.

'Not just now, sir,' Cheadle requested. 'And if you must, not here.'

'Now,' Mark insisted. 'And here. I want my brother to know the facts' – glacing at Robbie. Even managing a smile. Which Robbie could not return. 'Ready, Sergeant?'

The sergeant for once looked uncertain as to how to proceed.

'Take it down,' Cheadle growled.

'Christ!' groaned Robbie, and wheeled himself to the garden doorway, his back to them all.

'I, Marcus James Gifford,' Mark recited, 'of 11, Cornwall Crescent, London, S.W.5, being of sound mind hereby voluntarily confess to the murders of four girls since August of last year. I also confess to the attempted murder of my brother last night, Thursday the – What's the date?'

Amused, Robbie looked round. And interrupted. 'Mark?'

'Yes.'

'I *wanted* to die. On Wednesday I good as told you.'

'I know.'

'And last night, when I asked you to pour me a nightcap. . . .'

'I know that too.'

'Only I lost my nerve.'

'You don't have to explain.'

'To you, perhaps not,' Cheadle corrected. 'But to me, he does. Why did you want your brother to kill you, Mr Robert?'

'He was your only witness,' Mark intervened, 'He wanted to deny you that witness.'

'Mark?' Robbie again. No longer cavalier. Almost timid, in fact. And sagging, his authority gone.

'Yes?'

'You believe me?'

'I believe you.'

'I'm sorry I locked my door.'

Mark smiled. 'I couldn't have done it even if you hadn't.'

For the first time in twelve years they were really close; and unembarrassed by their closeness. Robbie laughed, arm on diaphragm, and sat erect again. 'Useless pair, aren't we? I couldn't either. Just waved me sword and chuntered on about how I'd suffered before you were even born. Strange.'

'Forget it, Robbie.'

'No. Whatever happens, you remember it.'

Cheadle decided it was time to start juggling again. 'I don't want to interrupt this very personal exchange, gentlemen; but may we now, Mr Mark, have the rest of your confession?'

Robbie turned away, only vaguely aware that Mark had answered, 'The rest?'

'There are a few details outstanding.'

'Such as?'

'The murder weapon.'

'Oh – one of Robbie's old sabres.'

'Where is it?'

'In the garage.'

'Thank you, sir,' said Cheadle courteously. And withdrawing the warrant from his inside pocket, clearing his throat, declaimed: '*Robert Stephen* Gifford, I have here a warrant—'

'But I've confessed! shouted Mark, leaping from his

chair, standing guard between the police and Robbie, his hand on Robbie's shoulder.

'To murdering four girls with a sabre?' Cheadle queried.

'Yes.'

'That was not the weapon employed,' Cheadle told him. 'Not that we know exactly what it was, but it wasn't a blade, and whatever it was, we're certain your brother used it.'

Having disposed of Mark, he bent his gaze upon the nape of Robbie's neck. A muscular neck. Too good for lesions. Come on, clever Master Robert. Admit it. Admit that you've met your match.

Robbie slewed accusingly round in his chair. 'You don't play bridge at all, do you, copper?'

'No, sir. But in my younger days I did use to juggle.'

'Good God,' exclaimed Robbie. And turning his back on them all once more, allowed his head to sink on his chest.

Mark moved his hand from his brother's shoulder to his neck, massaging gently, still standing guard, disliking Cheadle for the zeal with which he hunted, taking no pains to conceal his dislike.

'As we see it, sir,' Cheadle told him, 'your brother hoped we'd suspect you each time a girl was murdered. He picked each of them up about an hour before you'd told him you'd be arriving, and disposed of each of them, except the last, when you were en route to your cousins. As a cripple he was not a likely suspect—'

'Still isn't,' Mark reminded.

'Not a likely one, no. But not an impossible one. You, however, were.'

'Until the Rex I may have been. . . .'

'Even the Rex didn't qualify you for the rôle of Motorway Maniac.'

'Why not?'

'The P & O Company tell me anatomy is not a subject taught to officers of the Merchant Marine.'

'I don't get the relevance.'

'The relevance of a knowledge of anatomy to the identity of the Motorway Maniac is that only someone with a thorough grasp of that very un-nautical subject could have killed all four girls with an identical upwards, right-handed thrust from just below the centre of the rib cage. Your brother's right handed; and the Middlesex Medical School tell us he was brilliant at anatomy.'

'Has the Middlesex Medical School produced only one right handed student who was brilliant at anatomy?' Mark countered. 'And is the Middlesex the only medical school that produces brilliant students? And why would anyone brilliant fumble his fourth murder if he'd succeeded with his first three?'

'Your brother became impatient, sir. He had to trap you this time or not at all, because, as you yourself were about to remark a minute ago, only you bit it back, he's less than a year to. . . .'

'Don't!' Mark begged. 'Please!'

'He knows, sir,' Cheadle insisted, 'Dr Fairburn told us your brother knows those lesions will kill him within the year.' He shook his head. 'Ironic, isn't it? He claims he got them lifting a rented TV. Only he never did rent a TV. So how *did* he get 'em? Shoving bodies out of his car.'

Cheadle made it sound like something by Euclid. Looked as if he he were about to say Q.E.D. Was gazing at Mark with almost academic pleasure, defying him to disprove what had been so logically demonstrated.

Still massaging Robbie's neck, very cool now that he knew the nature of the problem confronting him, Mark said : 'You've got your data wrong. The only body you're sure about was in *my* car, not his.'

'Put there by him,' agreed Cheadle condescendingly. 'Impossible.'

'The wheelmarks of his chair prove it. After all that rain on Wednesday, the lawn was soft. Wherever your brother moved, he left tracks. They're still there, sir. The shallower ones where he wheeled only himself : the deeper ones where he wheeled an extra burden of about a hundred and twenty pounds. We've done tests. And Janine Talbot weighed a hundred and nineteen pounds.'

'Someone else could have put her in my car.'

'Someone else in a wheelchair? Someone else with a knowledge of anatomy? Someone else who hated you enough to frame you and kill you, and make us believe it was suicide? Someone else who despised policemen so much he incorporated into his plot a gambit that made them a laughing stock throughout the country?'

'What gambit?'

'Dumping three of his victims outside Police Stations. The Press loved that.'

'You can't prove he despises policemen.'

'His attitude towards us since Wednesday?'

'The attitude of an innocent citizen whose home you'd invaded.'

Cheadle shook his head. 'He led us here. He thrust a scent under our noses. A very relevant scene to which he subsequently and repeatedly drew my attention by calling it custard and my sergeant a poof.'

'Doesn't prove him a murderer.'

'He also,' Cheadle expatiated, 'hates scrubbers.'

'Not partial to them myself,' Mark retorted.

'But you didn't have one for a mother.'

'You saying all scrubber's sons are murders?'

'Mr Mark,' Cheadle sighed, 'are you saying that you are still the Motorway Maniac?'

'Aren't you forgetting the scrubber *I* picked up?'

'She came to see us yesterday. Told us she'd been picked up at ten to three and dropped off at five past. Gave us a good description of you, sir : as did her aunt, who was waiting for her outside the Aylesbury Post Office.'

It was the alibi he'd always known he could call upon if it had come to a trial. Knowing that, he'd been prepared to risk a trial : to give Robbie time.

But now that his alibi pointed to Robbie as a murderer, he almost wished he'd never had one. Just as Robbie had wished he hadn't had one. Had been so shaken by the realization that he might have one that he'd been unable to refrain from question after question as to whether anyone outside the Post Office had seen him 'put down' his blonde nympho.

Which was the moment, Mark reflected, he'd known for sure what he'd suspected the moment he saw Janine Talbot's body sprawled along the front seat of his car : that his brother was a killer who'd shouted angrily rather than allow whisky to be collected from a car parked next to his own, and been downright rude rather than allow his bow and arrows to be carried out to his own car, in which lay his latest victim.

Mark allowed his hand to fall from his brother's neck. Everything Cheadle said was true : even that the purpose of all the murders was so to incriminate him that he too could be murdered. Otherwise, why had Robbie put him in a position where he had to dispose of a body? Otherwise, why – when the body had been disposed of – had Robbie not accepted that service with gratitude? Why, instead, had he insisted that they return to the Rex?

All along it could only have been Robbie, and he'd known it; but been unable to reconcile himself to that knowledge.

Even now he felt obliged to protest. 'He couldn't

have . . . I mean, even if he'd wanted to—' That was the thing he couldn't accept : that Robbie should have wanted to kill. 'He *couldn't* have done it,' he muttered.

'That why you tried to persuade his doctor to recall him to hospital?' Cheadle enquired. 'Because he couldn't have done it? Or because you knew he had, and wanted him somewhere where he couldn't do it again?'

'I'm sorry' – Mark looked stubborn – 'it's all too circumstantial.'

'Not all,' Cheadle contradicted, 'What would you say if I told you we found traces of Janine Talbot's blood on the seat of his car?'

From Robbie, then, came his only comment on their long dialogue : a sardonic snort of laughter.

Cheadle threw an enigmatic glance at the bowed head : then, almost sympathetically, enquired : 'May we dispense with your confession now, Mr Mark?'

Standing with his back to Robbie's chair, Mark shrugged.

'I had to give him time.'

'That, I understand, sir; but his time is run out and he is a murderer.'

'You don't know him.'

'Enough to appreciate that he hated his mother for forsaking him, us for not nicking his mother, and you for coming between him and his adoptive parents. Of course that's an over-simplification; but explaining to a jury your brother's motive for murders done and attempted won't, I'm happy to say, be my job. And now, sir' – once again displaying his warrant – 'if I may?'

Mark moved round Robbie's chair, to face and comfort his brother; and Cheadle began to intone.

'Robert Stephen Gifford' he charged. But stopped as he saw Mark's hand dart to Robbie's chest, saw the look on his face, heard him saying 'Save your breath, Chief

Superintendent,' and saw the weapon embedded beneath Robbie's ribs as the wheelchair was whirled to confront him.

Throwing aside his note book, the sergeant leaped to the wheelchair. Hand on Robbie's wrist, head then to his heart, he searched for any sign of life.

'Gone?' asked Cheadle, rhetorically, laconically almost. The sergeant nodded.

'Poor Robbie,' Mark muttered, turning his back.

Cheadle advanced slowly and peered down at the cloth-bound haft protruding from Robbie's chest. 'So that's the murder weapon. Half an arrow. I suppose we should have guessed.' He put the warrant back in his pocket. 'Wheel Mr Gifford to his bedroom, will you, Sergeant? He always hated being gawped at.' Mark turned and watched as his brother was wheeled away.

'There are a few things more we must discuss, sir,' Cheadle told him. 'But first, I think, you should have a cup of tea. May I?' Nodding at the kitchen.

Blindly, Mark waved his assent; and stolidly Cheadle filled the kettle.

FRIDAY: HALF PAST FIVE

Cheadle was looking round the kitchen when the sergeant
returned from Robbie's bedroom.

'Excuse me, Mr Gifford,' said Cheadle, 'but where
will I find the crockery?'

'What? Oh – teaspoons in the top drawer, cups and
saucers in the second and teapot in the third. Drawers
are – were – easier than cupboards for . . . for my brother.'

'Of course.' But Mark was no longer listening, had
looked away, did not see the sergeant hand his superior
an envelope.

After a moment's thought, Cheadle said: 'A letter for
you, sir. From your brother, I suspect.' Handing it back
to the sergeant, he nodded permission for it to be passed
to Mark. 'Afraid I'll have to read it too; but if you'd like
a few moments alone . . . ?'

Shaking his head, Mark opened the envelope.

The first he's ever written me, he thought; and I don't
want to read it.

Little brother, Mark read, while the sergeant rang for
an ambulance, *if you get to read this, I'll be dead instead
of you. And if you're not dead, it will be because I've
been sitting up all night remembering everything you've
ever done for me and doubting my hatred of you for the
first time. I even began to wonder whether I didn't feel
for you as one brother should for another.*

155

I even forgot, for a few hours, that I was never quite sure of the parental love you never doubted.

I even forgot, for a few hours, all those times you called me into the bathroom here to talk to you while you showered; and how, each time I sat impotent in my chair, watching you stretch and stoop and soap yourself, I detested you for your blatant virility.

For a few hours, I even doubted the sanity of the end I've planned for you. Right now, though (because I'm remembering those showers, and those girl friends in London you've always denied, and those shipboard romances you'll never discuss) I'm hating you; but doubt is a strange thing. At least, it's a stranger to me.

So who knows, doubt having once unsettled me, that I won't get unsettled again tomorrow, when I plan to kill you? Certainly, if I don't do it quickly, I'll never do it.

Should that happen, and you get to read this letter, (which God forbid) there are a few things you might like to know.

First, why was I so rattled when you arrived early on Wednesday? Because it was raining when I got back with the girl, which meant I couldn't spend five minutes in the open wiping her grubby prints off the door and anything else she might have touched. I can't afford to get wet; and I had to leave the car on the drive so that later I could transfer the girl to your car. No room for such antics in the garage.

So the car stayed in the rain and I came inside, to wait till the rain stopped. But just as the rain stopped, you arrived! I was very put out.

As to how I killed each time. I simply dawdled up and down the A.41 till I saw a likely girl, stopped and unlatched the door. I said nothing and didn't even look at her. But if she got in, she had only one chance of staying alive; to resist when I put my hand on her sternum (look it up!) and started kissing her.

None of them did. All four closed their eyes and kissed back. I kept my eye on the place where my hand had been, took a bit of old arrow out of the glove box and bashed it home.

Each died kissing me. And before you judge me, let me ask you again, what were they really looking for, those girls who found me?

Finally, how did I plan to involve you? Simply by telephoning from Stoke and asking you to buy the vegetables I'd 'forgotten' to buy for dinner. You'd have gone out to your car, found the girl and either got rid of her, called the Police, or waited to ask my advice. Whichever, I'd have contrived to incriminate you enough to make your subsequent suicide feasible.

But when I did phone, you were out already, on your way to the Rex, which was utterly unexpected, but has made everything much more exciting since.

That's all I can tell you. I know it doesn't answer the biggest question of all: Did I kill just to implicate you, or for the pleasure of killing as well? I thought I knew. Now I'm not sure.

I wish I could say something to comfort you if I don't kill you; but the kindest truth I can offer is that last night, for a few hours, I quite liked you. A few hours in twenty-five years isn't much, I know, but better perhaps than nothing.

You're banging on my door again. Whichever way this goes, at least, little brother, you'll see no more of

Yours treacherously,
Robbie Thomson.

Mark put down the letter and stared into the empty

fireplace. Cheadle handed him a cup of tea and left him
to his thoughts until the cup was empty.

'A bit better now, sir?' he asked then.

Mark nodded. 'You want this? – offering the letter.

'Afraid I must, sir' – taking it and lowering himself into
an arm-chair.

Having read it, he too stared into the fire-place. Then
said: 'He was fonder of you than he was prepared to
admit.'

'What makes you say that?'

'He signs himself Thomson. *Your* name's mentioned
nowhere.'

'Read it again!'

'I don't need to. He refers to you throughout as "little
brother". Cheer up, sir. You're young and alive.'

'I feel old and dead.'

'That'll pass.'

I wonder, thought Mark. Then wondered aloud:
'Would he have killed me?'

'He had his chance, didn't he?'

Mark remembered the long minutes of his final con-
frontation with Robbie, felt again the sabre pricking at
his chest, saw again the sudden emergence of Cheadle
from the hall way.

'He'd locked himself in and I'd been out to look
through his window. That's why the front door was open.
Why'd he . . . why did he kill all those girls?'

'I don't know, Mr Gifford. Our psychiatrist has some
theories, of course. They always do, don't they? Mr
Robert's mother – his real mother, I mean – was a blonde
and a whore and twenty-three years old when last he
saw her: our psychiatrist suggests he might have been
murdering her each time.'

'You said it was so he could murder me.'

'And I know how our psychiatrist would answer that.

He'd say Mr Robert would convince himself he was plotting to destroy you, with whom there was no blood tie,
rather than admit to matricide.'

'There's a hell of a gap between plotting and actually
killing.'

'His father, sir was XYY,' advised Cheadle; as if that
explained everything.'

'What's that?' asked Mark, to whom it explained
nothing.

'A chromosomatic abnormality frequently found in very
big, very strong, very violent men. Some, like our psychiatrist, even believe it to be an abnormality which *in-
duces* violence.'

'Is Robbie . . . was Robbie XYY?'

'No idea, sir. But his father's at present doing fourteen
years for grievous bodily harm – his fifth conviction in
twenty-seven years; of which he's spent only two *out* of
gaol – so probably your brother didn't have much of a
chance.'

Mark thought of the last chance adoption had offered
his brother, and muttered : 'I wish I'd never been born.'

'You mustn't think that,' Cheadle rebuked. 'It's silly,
it does no good and anyway it was a circumstance over
which you had no control.'

'Needn't have invited him into the bathroom, though,
need I?'

'What's done is done, sir,' said Cheadle primly.

'I never thought. After boarding school, and life at
sea. . . . I suppose I should have; but I never thought.
We'd always talked in the bathroom.'

Cheadle was relieved to hear it. The bathroom para-
graph had bothered him. He would never have showered
in front of another man. Indecent. But as Mark explained
it merely immodest. 'I don't think it'd have made a blind
bit of difference if you'd gone bathless these past six

years. In fact, for once I'm inclined to agree with our psychiatrist : your brother wanted to be caught. Bodies in front of police stations; dragging you back to the Rex. Didn't you *know* you stank of perfume?'

'I couldn't smell it any longer.'

'And the way he practically told us how the job at the Rex was done. Is a man who does all those things trying to get away with it?'

'If it's a challenge he's issuing, maybe he is.'

'Well, if that's what he was up to, he was on a hiding to nothing the moment I learnt he'd never rented a TV; and it had to be a hiding the moment he assured me there'd have been no more Motorway Murders once you were dead. That gave us his motive for all the killings. To incriminate you.'

'And what now?' Mark demanded. 'A blaze of publicity about Robert Gifford, the Wheel Chair Murderer?'

Cheadle shook his head. 'A coroner's enquiry into the death of a Mr X who left a suicide letter confessing to the four murders of the Motorway Maniac.'

Mark frowned, both perplexed and suspicious. 'Why?'

'The Giffords are blameless. He acknowledged that when he signed himself Thomson. Also, of course, one wants to protect the Stoke Mandeville image. They're remarkable people.'

Again Mark frowned; but this time with surprise. His own efforts to protect Robbie had been less altruistic.

'If it's just a Mr X who's committed suicide,' he pointed out, 'everyone'll think you'd never have caught him; that you're just a stupid copper—'

'Mr Gifford, ask a hundred thousand people the day after tomorrow who led the fourteen months' enquiry into these murders, not more than two'll be able to tell you. And both of them'll be villains!'

'And what about me?'

'I hope you've understood why I acted as I did.'

'I meant, what are you going to do about me? I've helped a murderer, obstructed you, made a false confession—'

'He was a born manipulator,' said Cheadle tolerantly. Mark shook his head. 'Not born.'

Cheadle looked curious. 'Did he never discuss it with you, sir? I mean, openly?'

'Oh yes. Since yesterday he's referred to us constantly as the Maniac and his Witness.'

'Which you accepted?'

'He said it was up to me – I could ring you any time I liked and put an end to it.'

'All manipulators have confidence in their superior will, Mr Gifford.'

It was an observation Mark found himself unable to dispute. By sheer will power Robbie had kept him away from both cars until Janine Talbot's body had been transferred from the one to the other.

'Was she under his dashboard when I got here on Wednesday?' Mark wondered.

'Now how did you know that?'

'Paraplegics don't have foot controls in their cars. Jesus, no wonder he. . . . When I went out to get some whisky she was on my front seat. I thought then . . . I thought, it must be him. That I had to. . . . I couldn't just turn him in.'

'As you said, sir, he needed time.'

'May I stay till the ambulance comes? See him into it?'

'Travel with him, if you like. Though if you take my advice, you'll say goodbye to him here.'

'Yes.' Mark cleared his throat. 'When will you be charging me?'

'Sir?' Cheadle looked extravagantly blank.

'I was an accessory,' Mark reminded. 'To the murder of Janine Talbot. Remember?'

Apparently bemused, Cheadle turned to his sergeant for advice: then, getting none, back to Mark. 'No, sir, I don't remember that. Do you remember that, Sergeant?' The sergeant, on the contrary, looked amnesiac. 'Sergeant doesn't either, sir. What can you be talking about? The only accessory we remember is that long haired laddie from Scotland. Who's vanished! London, I suppose. Dead by now, quite likely. Heroin, amphetamines; all the same, these hippies.'

The door bell rang.

'That will be the ambulance, Sergeant. Tell them just to put Mr Robert on a stretcher in his bedroom and wait outside will you?' Though content with his quarry's demise, Cheadle was anxious that the dead should seem peaceful in death, not hunted.

The sergeant departed; and Cheadle collected all the tea cups and took them to the sink, where, methodically, he rinsed them and stacked them on the draining board. The sergeant returned.

'Mr Gifford?' Cheadle called. Mark looked up. 'If you'd like to see your brother . . . ?'

'Yes, thank you.'

He walked slowly to Robbie's room; and, entering it, stared down at the stretcher.

Lying on his back, blanket-covered except for his face, Robbie, in death, betrayed none of the horror of his life. His legs could have been the legs of a man who walked. His death could have been the sleep of a saint. His expression was serene.

So serene that Mark was compelled to look again. And to discern not serenity but emptiness. An emptiness he'd observed only once before – in the clear eyes of a young sailor arrested for the murder of a fellow seaman. An emptiness that had explained nothing, because what the young sailor had done was meaningless : that had concealed nothing, because behind his eyes was only emotional emptiness.

One might as well grieve for a butterfly transfixed to a board : say goodbye to a Warhol on a gallery wall : regret lost innocence.

Looking down at the empty face, Mark whispered : 'Goodbye, Robbie' – and returned to Cheadle.

'We'll be on our way, sir,' Cheadle told him then.

'Yes.'

'You'll not be required at the inquest.'

'Thank you.'

Cheadle hesitated, then held out his hand. 'If we meet again, I hope it'll be in happier circumstances.'

'Yes.' Shaking the hunter's hand : being polite to a superior officer.

'Come on, Sergeant.'

Mutely, the sergeant inclined his head, turned and departed.

About to follow him, Cheadle hesitated again. 'Er . . . should the subject of accessories to the murder of Miss Talbot ever arise, sir, you won't forget what I told you, will you ?'

'No.' Obliging himself to the hunter : condoning what the hunter had done : ashamed.

'Goodbye, Mr Gifford.'

'Goodbye.'

He stood quite still. Heard the front door shut. Heard the ambulance doors shut. Heard the car doors shut. Heard ambulance and police car drive down the narrow lane. And, looking slowly round the comfortable, meaningless room – meaningless as Robbie – wept.

FRIDAY: FIVE TO SIX

As they swung right into the road to Aylesbury, the sergeant glanced at his superior: a questioning glance, inviting comment. From the corner of his eye, Cheadle caught the question; and ignored it.

The sergeant coughed, making clearer his desire for communication; and Cheadle ignored him again.

The sergeant gripped the steering wheel momentarily tighter, relaxed his grip, lifted his head high and said: 'Sir?' His accent was pure Oxbridge, but nervous.

Cheadle slid low on the seat, tired and reluctant. 'What is it, Sergeant?'

'I have the feeling, sir,' the sergeant replied, 'that in the matter of the death of Mr Robert Gifford, his brother Mark was not alone in his determination to give the deceased, I quote, "time".'

Cheadle shoved himself irritably upright.

'Sergeant, I'm a tired, simple man: forget your degrees, spare me your circumlocutions, and speak to me simply.'

'Yes, sir. Putting it simply, for two days I think you've been offering Robert Gifford time to make a choice.'

'Between what and what?'

'Between life in an institution for the criminally insane, sir, and death by his own hand,' said the sergeant with considerable courage.

164

Cheadle gave a sardonic grunt. 'That's a very serious allegation, Sergeant.'

'I've worked with you a long time, sir : I know your usual methods.'

'Mr Gifford wasn't one to be trapped by the usual methods,' Cheadle growled.

'His thinking *was* rather lateral, sir.'

'That what you call it?'

'But so was yours, sir. You *seemed* to be saying, "Mr Gifford, why not be your own executioner?" '

Cheadle jerked erect : 'Pull up!' he ordered. The sergeant brought the car smoothly to a halt, frightened now, his eyes on the road ahead as Cheadle slewed round to confront him.

'You seriously believe,' Cheadle demanded, 'that I wanted Robert Thomson to kill himself?'

'Yes, sir.' Eyes still front.

'And assuming that I did, would society scream because he obliged me?'

'No, sir. Society'd say nothing; be grateful he was dead.'

Cheadle slumped back in his seat. 'All hypocrites, aren't we?' He stared moodily through the windscreen. 'Want to know something? I *liked* Master Robert. Knew he was a murderer; but liked him. Liked him; but gave him time to kill himself.'

'It was a compassionate solution, sir.' Aware that he lied : that Cheadle was impelled by a need to destroy criminals that had nothing to do with either the Law or criminality : that Cheadle was as much a stranger to compassion as any murderer.

'Compassionate, balls. If I'd arrested him, he'd have got off. He knew that. It's what he meant when he said he was calling a grand slam in spades. He was telling me he was a killer I couldn't convict.'

166

'*Would* he have got off, sir?'

'Certainly. Defence counsel would have accused his brother – dead or alive – of being the real murderer. They'd have shown that the only place Mr Mark could previously have seen a bit of that Fellini film, for example, was the Rex. It's never been shown on the Canberra. They'd have shown that the only convincing motive was money: Mr Mark's money that Mr Robert was spending like water. They'd have tied in knots the girl who gave Mr Mark his alibi – and her aunty. They'd have shown Mr Mark had equal opportunity, was a more likely murderer than a cripple and was the only man who could've left the Talbot lass at the Rex. They'd have got the jury so confused they'd have been unable to decide that Mr Robert was guilty beyond all reasonable doubt. Oh – he'd have got off all right.'

'Then why did he kill himself?'

'Because the whole cunning plot fell apart in his hands when he found he couldn't kill his brother. Denied that end, all his murders became not just means to an end but the vicious work of a maniac. That's what I had to show him. He knew it of course; but it had to be spelt out to him. So I obliged him. I spelt it out. You're a sick, murderous maniac, I spelt out to him. Then gave him time to kill himself.'

'Yes, sir.' The sergeant's expression had become less certain than ever.

'But?' prompted Cheadle.

'But *I* think he might *not* have killed himself.'

'He *might* not have,' agreed Cheadle.

'He could have, of course: when you told him we'd found traces of the girl's blood on the seat of his car, and he laughed.' The sergeant thumped his diaphragm to indicate how Robbie could have killed himself. 'But his brother could've done it just as feasibly: when you started

reading the charge, and his hand flashed to Mr Robert's
chest.'

'Only to snatch out a bit of arrow, surely?'

'Or plunge it in.'

Cheadle nodded fatalistically. 'Could've been up the
sleeve of either, of course: waiting. Towelling handle.
No fingerprints.' He dug in his pocket for a handkerchief
and blew his nose.

'Was it suicide, sir?' the sergeant persisted.

'Suicide, fracticide! Quibbles, Sergeant. It was my kind
of judicial homicide.'

'Put it like that, sir, society *will* scream.'

'But I shan't put it like that. You're the only ideallist
likely to put it like that.'

'Me, sir?' – looking straight at Cheadle.

'You're the one who knows we found no blood on the
seat of Master Robert's car. You're the one who knows
that my hint that we had was what finally broke Master
Robert's will. And you're the one who'll be a witness
tomorrow at the coroner's enquiry into the death of Master
Robert. So when your turn comes to give evidence, how
will you put it, my learned, liberal-minded friend?'

The sergeant stared blankly through the windscreen,
thinking about the cunning with which Cheadle had said,
'What would you say *if I told you* we'd found traces of
Janine Talbot's blood on the front seat of his car?'

Thinking about Truth, and Justice – and promotion.

And mindful of Cheadle's ruthlessness, of the fact that
it was *he*, not Cheadle, who'd smelt Janine Talbot's perfume on Mark Gifford and of the promotion that meant
so much to him, he intoned :

'I saw the deceased slide something out of his right
sleeve and, gripping it firmly with his right hand, drive
it upwards into his abdomen. I rushed to his assistance;
but he was dead.'

Cheadle nodded his approval. 'Then society'll be happy, won't it?'

'Yes, sir. But just between ourselves, did he do it: or did his brother do it to him?'

'Just between ourselves, Sergeant,' rumbled Cheadle, eyes closed, 'it no longers matters.'